"Shall I tell you what I'm really thinking?" he asked softly.

"I'm thinking you have the most beautiful mouth I've ever seen. I'm thinking that I very badly want to kiss you."

A sharp thrill of pleasure coursed through her at his words, but she fought to deny it. She reminded herself that Steve was a federal agent and that, as far as she was concerned, he was little better than her jailer. But somehow the reminder seemed unimportant in comparison with the way he made her feel.

Hesitantly she traced his mouth with her thumb. His lips felt firm and cool beneath her fingers. When her thumb finally halted at the corner of his mouth, he turned his face toward her hand and pressed a single hard kiss against the pulse beating in her wrist.

The shock of pleasure was so intense that she shivered...

"Steve, we can't do this," she said. "This is insane. It's crazy." She gave a tiny gasp of laughter. "It's probably even illegal."

"Do you think I don't know that?" His words were no more than a harsh murmur against the palm of her hand...

Dear Reader:

Three months ago we were delighted to announce the arrival of TO HAVE AND TO HOLD, the thrilling new romance series that takes you into the world of married love. We're pleased to report that letters of praise and enthusiasm are pouring in daily. TO HAVE AND TO HOLD is clearly off to a great start!

TO HAVE AND TO HOLD is the first and only series that portrays the joys and heartaches of marriage. Its unique concept makes it significantly different from the other lines now available to you, and it presents stories that meet the high standards set by SECOND CHANCE AT LOVE. TO HAVE AND TO HOLD offers all the compelling romance, exciting sensuality, and heartwarming entertainment you expect.

We think you'll love TO HAVE AND TO HOLD—and that you'll become the kind of loyal reader who is making SECOND CHANCE AT LOVE an ever-increasing success. Read about love affairs that last a lifetime. Look for three TO HAVE AND TO HOLD romances each and every month, as well as six SECOND CHANCE AT LOVE romances each month. We hope you'll read and enjoy them all. And please keep writing! Your thoughts about our books are very important to us.

Warm wishes,

Ellen Edwards

Ellen Edwards
SECOND CHANCE AT LOVE
The Berkley Publishing Group
200 Madison Avenue
New York, N.Y. 10016

REFUGE IN HIS ARMS
JASMINE CRAIG

A SECOND CHANCE AT LOVE BOOK

Other Second Chance at Love books by
Jasmine Craig

TENDER TRIUMPH	#29
RUNAWAY LOVE	#46
STORMY REUNION	#80
IMPRISONED HEART	#118

REFUGE IN HIS ARMS

Copyright © 1984 by Jasmine Craig

Distributed by The Berkley Publishing Group

All rights reserved. No part of this publication may be reproduced or transmitted in any form or by any means, electronic or mechanical, including photocopy, recording, or any information storage and retrieval system, without permission in writing from the publisher.

Requests for permission to make copies of any part of the work should be mailed to: Permissions, Second Chance at Love, The Berkley Publishing Group, 200 Madison Avenue, New York, NY 10016.

First edition published January 1984

First printing

"Second Chance at Love" and the butterfly emblem are trademarks belonging to Jove Publications, Inc.

Printed in the United States of America

Second Chance at Love books are published by
The Berkley Publishing Group
200 Madison Avenue, New York, NY 10016

REFUGE IN HIS ARMS

Chapter One

MEGAN WAS RINSING her coffee cup when the front doorbell rang. The mug slipped through her fingers and shattered against the side of the sink. She didn't stop to pick up the pieces. She grabbed a kitchen towel and wiped her hands feverishly as she ran through the living room. Perhaps Jeffrey had come back to tell her it was all a mistake. Perhaps he hadn't deliberately set out to deceive her. Maybe he had never intended to humiliate her so completely.

When she reached the tiny entrance hall, her hands were still shaking, and she had trouble turning the old-fashioned lock. She finally managed to open the door and saw two men standing on the doorstep. Neither of them was Jeffrey.

For a split second she was afraid she might burst into tears. Then the self-control she had learned during her lonely childhood quickly reasserted itself. She managed to twist her mouth into a polite smile. "Hello," she said, keeping her voice as calm as her expression. "Can I help you?"

The older of the two men was a bit heavy-set. He pulled at his collar before stepping forward. "Is this twenty-nine Hunter Lane?" he asked courteously. "The Brookfield residence?"

"Yes, yes it is." She was surprised at his question, and she scrutinized the pair more closely. Neither of them, she realized, looked in the least like a door-to-door salesman, but she couldn't imagine who else would call on her at this hour of the morning.

The taller man, in fact, didn't look at all friendly, although she noticed in a distracted sort of way that he was very good-looking. He was at least six feet tall, powerfully built, his complexion tanned and his hair bleached a streaky blond by the sun. His eyes were dark blue. And cold, she thought, turning away from the grimness of his expression. He was looking at her as though she'd just crawled out from under some dark, slimy stone. No, these men were certainly not trying to sell her anything.

A sudden explosion of fear overcame her wariness. "What's happened?" she asked. "Who are you?"

The men exchanged a swift, silent glance before the one who had already spoken said, "Are you Megan Brookfield?"

"Yes, I am. What do you want?"

"We want to talk to your husband, Mrs. Brookfield. Is he at home?"

Refuge In His Arms

She drew in a deep breath, then let it out very slowly. "Who are you?" she asked again. "Why are you asking so many questions?"

"I'm a police officer, Mrs. Brookfield. My associate and I want to have a word with your husband. It's rather urgent."

"Police officers!" She glanced unseeingly at the card the British policeman held in front of her. She felt sure her cheeks had turned white. Was it possible that Jeffrey had played one final cruel trick on her? Had he alerted the police to the truth before disappearing? Had he confessed to committing the crime of bigamy and then run out, leaving her to face the consequences? She stared down at the floor, trying to hide her concern. "Wh–what's happened?" she asked "Why do you want to speak to Jeffrey? I'm afraid he isn't here right now."

The tall, good-looking man spoke for the first time. "We think Dr. Brookfield can help us with an investigation we're conducting," he said tersely. "Do you know when your husband will return? It's important for us to get in touch with him as soon as possible."

She looked up, unable to hide her astonishment. "You're American!" she exclaimed.

"Yes, I am. And so are you, Mrs. Brookfield. Now would you please answer my questions?"

Her face grew hot, but she bit back the angry retort that hovered on the tip of her tongue. She wondered why the American seemed to dislike her, when they had never seen each other until this moment. She also wondered what on earth an American police officer was doing in England. However, she wasn't going to ask him and risk another snub. She had no interest in the policemen; she simply wanted to get rid of them.

"I'm sorry, but I'm afraid I can't help you," she repeated. "My husb—Jeffrey is away on a business trip, and I'm not sure when he'll be back."

"His business has taken him overseas, no doubt," the American said, and she could still hear a disturbing note of derision in his voice.

She had no idea where Jeffrey was, but pride prevented her from admitting the truth. "Yes," she said, wondering even as she spoke if it was a crime to lie to police officers. "He's traveling around Europe."

"How inconvenient that you don't have an address for him. Or convenient, I guess, depending on your point of view."

She was suddenly frightened by the strange persistence of the two policemen. "I'm sorry I have nothing useful to tell you," she said, getting ready to close the door.

"But *we* think you have the information we need, Mrs. Brookfield. Are you sure you don't know how we can reach your husband?"

"Yes, I've already told you I'm quite sure!" Her nerves were strung tight after a sleepless night, and she desperately wanted to be alone to decide how she was going to put the pieces of her life back together. She realized suddenly that the American police officer was watching her intently, and she forced her fears back behind a blank mask. As a child she had learned to protect herself by hiding her emotions, and recently she had become an expert at concealing her true feelings.

She managed to produce another polite smile. "I'm afraid I'm very busy, so if you'll excuse me..." She tried to close the front door, but, to her horror, the American leaned his shoulder against it and forcibly prevented it from closing.

"Get out!" she said, attempting to push the door shut. "Get out! You have no right to force your way into my home!"

"We have a search warrant," he said. "Wait!" With his free hand he reached into his jacket pocket and extracted a small plastic card. "I'm sure you've guessed which agency we're from, but British law requires me to show my identification before we come in." He held the card at arm's length, directly in Megan's line of vision.

She glanced at the card, trying to absorb the meaning of the words embossed on the white plastic surface. The tiny letters blurred in front of her eyes, refusing to form themselves into believable phrases. She closed her eyes for a moment, but when she looked at the card for the second time, it still bore the same incredible information. Steven M. Callahan was an agent of the United States government, currently on an overseas assignment with the Central Intelligence Agency.

"A federal agent from the CIA?" she said, fright reducing her voice to a husky whisper. "Why should somebody from the CIA want to talk to Jeffrey? He's never even visited the States."

For some incomprehensible reason the CIA agent's expression seemed to become even more derisive. "I'm sorry if we've alarmed you," he said with mock courtesy, "but I think it would be better if we continued this conversation inside. By the way, I had the impression you didn't read my colleague's identification card. This is Inspector Sidney Browning. He's attached to the Special

Branch of Scotland Yard's Criminal Investigation Department."

"Scotland Yard?" she said faintly.

"Please take another look at my identification, Mrs. Brookfield," the inspector murmured. "And here is our search warrant."

Megan barely glanced at the documents he extended. "Tell me why you're here," she said. "Has something happened to somebody... to Jeffrey? Why won't you tell me what's happened?"

Both men looked at her. Neither seemed to show any trace of sympathy. "As far as we know, Dr. Brookfield is in excellent health," the inspector said. "But we could discuss this more satisfactorily if we came inside."

Steven Callahan's gaze flicked over her briefly. "You've already seen our search warrant, Mrs. Brookfield. You may as well let us in now as later."

She pressed her hand to her head and discovered she was still clutching the kitchen towel. She folded it neatly and put it on the hall table. "I guess you'd better come in," she said.

They followed her into the small living room of the cottage, and she knew she wasn't imagining the hostility that emanated from the American agent. She shivered with a touch of renewed fear. It required all of her willpower to stand in front of the empty fireplace and face them without showing any sign of intimidation. Surely they wouldn't assign a Scotland Yard inspector and an agent from the CIA to investigate a case of bigamy. Besides, she reminded herself, she was a victim, not a criminal. "I think it's time you told me exactly what you want from me," she said. "I want to know what this harassment is all about."

Steven Callahan looked at her silently, his gaze traveling over her in a slow, thorough examination. She resisted the urge to tug at the waistband of her cream wool sweater, but she couldn't prevent her shaky fingers from tucking one long, loose strand of dark hair back behind her ear. "We've told you what this is about, Mrs. Brookfield," Callahan said eventually. "We want to talk to your husband. Perhaps you can tell us when you expect him back."

During their brief time together Jeffrey had almost never been home. Megan had become so accustomed to saving her pride by lying about where he was that it ought to have been easy to toss off one more lie. Under Callahan's relentless stare, however, she found it unexpectedly difficult. "My... Jeffrey doesn't give me a minute-by-minute schedule," she said, as carelessly as she could. God knew, that was true enough. She kept her gaze focused somewhere near the inspector's chin. The lying was easier, for some reason, if she didn't run the risk of meeting Steven Callahan's eyes. "We both have careers, so Jeffrey knows I'm not sitting home waiting for him. I guess he'll give me a call when he arrives at the airport. So that I can fix dinner."

"Why aren't you at work today? I understand from your boss at the university library that you called in sick. Are you sick, Mrs. Brookfield?"

She discovered that her hand was twisting nervously through her hair again. She gave a casual flick to the heavy strands, then clasped her hands behind her back where nobody could see that they were shaking. "I had a migraine earlier this morning," she said.

"How lucky that it disappeared so soon! Perhaps you received a message from your husband that relieved your early morning tension, Mrs. Brookfield?"

Callahan's final piece of mockery was too much. "Why do you keep questioning me about Jeffrey?" she demanded. "What do you think I'm hiding from you? Do you think he's here? Is that why you keep asking me all these questions?"

"No," Callahan said. "That isn't why we've been questioning you."

She ignored his interruption, too angry and too emotionally wound up to maintain her usual calm demeanor. "Where do you think I've hidden him? Under the bed? Behind the sofa cushions?" In a burst of anger she began pulling the cushions off the sofa and tossing them haphazardly onto the floor.

"Surprise, surprise!" she said. "Jeffrey isn't here! But there's still the upstairs, gentlemen. Have a good look around, and don't forget the bedroom closet. Maybe I've hidden him between the spare blankets!"

"There's no need to upset yourself, Mrs. Brookfield," the inspector said quietly. "This is just part of a routine investigation. Nobody's accusing you of anything at the moment. Steve, do you want to take the bedrooms, and I'll look around down here?"

"Sure."

She felt her mouth fall open with astonishment. "You can't be serious!" she said. "You mean you expect me to let you walk into my home and paw through my personal belongings searching for Jeffrey? For heaven's sake, you can't possibly believe he's here!"

Steven Callahan looked at her, and the coolness of his gaze froze her into silence. "I think we all know where Jeffrey Brookfield is," he said. "Naturally, we're not looking for him here." He nodded briefly to the inspector. "I doubt we'll find anything at all, but we'll give it a shot. I'ts amazing how careless people can be when they leave in a hurry."

"Jeffrey didn't leave in a hurry," Megan said with a touch of bitterness. "He had everything planned."

The minute she spoke the words, she wished she had remained silent. Now she had pitched herself into just the sort of explanation she had wanted to avoid. Both men halted in their tracks, then turned to stare at her. "Please repeat what you just told us," Callahan said.

She shivered at the quiet menace implicit in his words. She turned away from him and walked to the window just so she would have something to look at other than his astonished, ferocious expression. "It was nothing important," she said, stumbling over the words. "I told you, Jeffrey left on a business trip. Of course he's been planning it for some time. You don't arrange business trips at the last minute."

"Your husband is a nuclear physicist, Mrs. Brookfield. A research scientist working for the government. Precisely what sort of a business trip was he planning? A sales trip?"

"Jeffrey and I didn't discuss his work," she mumbled, not prepared to admit to two total strangers that Jeffrey had left her permanently and that their marriage was nonexistent—a farce, an illegal fiction that Jeffrey had entered into for reasons she still totally failed to comprehend. Despite what she'd told the investigators, she had no idea whether he'd really gone away on business or whether, perhaps, he'd gone to rejoin his legal wife. She knew only that he hadn't been at the university lab when she'd swallowed her pride and called this morning. Yesterday evening, at the time of their final bitter argument, she hadn't thought to find out exactly where Jeffrey was going. Yesterday nothing had seemed to matter much except the fact that her marriage was irretrievably finished. Had never, in fact, begun because it had never been legal.

She became aware once again of the tense, expectant silence, and she lifted her chin defiantly as she turned to meet Callahan's piercing gaze. "Naturally Jeffrey didn't discuss his work with me. In the first place, his research is classified, and in the second place, I don't understand anything about nuclear physics. Our professional lives had nothing in common. I knew as little about the fusion of hydrogen atoms as he knew about the preservation of medieval manuscripts."

The inspector looked at her thoughtfully. "Why do you talk about your husband in the past tense, Mrs. Brookfield?"

She gasped, then began to laugh. "Oh, my God! Are you expecting to find his body stuffed in the bedroom closet? Is that what this is all about?"

Steven Callahan walked quickly to her side. "Sit down, Mrs. Brookfield," he said with unexpected gentleness. "Would you like a drink of water?"

She shook her head, but remained seated because it seemed easier than making yet another useless protest. The inspector spoke quietly to his colleague. "It seems pretty certain he was tipped off, don't you agree? Everything here seems remarkably tidy."

"We might be able to get a better idea when we look around the place." Callahan's expression was once again harsh as he turned toward Megan. "Depending of course, on how efficient his wife has been."

She forced herself to meet his gaze, but she said nothing. In truth, her mind was too dazed to think of anything logical to say. The two men left the room, and she heard the inspector as he moved around the kitchen, methodically opening and shutting drawers, poking around in cupboards. She thought with a touch of renewed hysteria that at least her high standard of housekeeping ought to impress him. Even Jeffrey had been pleased with her efficiency as a cook and cleaner. She wondered if his wife—his *real* wife—was equally as good.

The inspector made quite a lot of noise, but she couldn't hear much of what Callahan was doing. The bedroom was directly over the living room, but he moved quietly, and only an occasional muffled thump indicated that he was searching the upstairs every bit as methodically as Inspector Browning was searching the kitchen. She hated the thought of the minor secrets of her life being open to their inspection. Why should Inspector Browning be privileged to know that she bought Colombian coffee beans and ground them herself? Why should Steven Callahan learn that she wore a size 34C bra?

The inspector was still searching around—in her broom closet if the sounds were anything to go by—when Callahan returned to the living room. He carried her blue suitcase. "Planning on taking a trip, Mrs. Brookfield?" he asked. "I'm afraid you'll have to make other arrangements. There's no way you'll be leaving the neighborhood for a week or two."

Real fear for her personal safety seized Megan for the first time. True, these men had shown her I.D. cards. True, they'd waved a piece of paper in front of her, saying it was a search warrant. But what did she know about CIA methods of identification, or badges issued by Scotland Yard? For that matter, how would she know what a search warrant looked like?

"You can't stop me from going away for the weekend," she said with far more confidence than she felt. "I'm planning to meet an old college friend in London. She's in England only for a few days. It's crazy for you to say I can't leave."

"Not crazy, Mrs. Brookfield, merely a sensible precaution. And perfectly legal, I assure you. Perhaps your friend would be willing to visit you here." Steven Callahan turned away from her as soon as the inspector came into the living room. "Find anything?" he asked.

"No." The inspector shrugged. "It's been gone over by an expert. She's even vacuumed the broom cupboard. There's a broken cup in the sink, but she's washed the pieces clean. God knows why she didn't throw them away before we arrived. There's nothing in there that's any use to us."

"It's the same upstairs. Clean sheets on the bed, the old ones already laundered. The bathroom cabinet scrubbed with disinfectant. I guess she was up all night making sure there was nothing left. There isn't even one of his ties."

Megan got to her feet. Her stomach was churning, and her teeth were starting to chatter. "Get out!" she said. "Get out of my house right now."

"Sorry, ma'am, I'm sure you realize that we can't leave. You should have insisted on going with him."

She clamped her lips tightly shut to cut off the burst of hysterical laughter welling up in her throat. You should have gone with him, Callahan had said. If only he knew! If only Callahan knew what a ridiculous, humiliating farce her so-called marriage had been. "I want to be left alone," she said fiercely, fighting to keep the panic out of her voice. It required a tremendous effort to force her voice under control, and the sickness in her stomach increased. "How do I know you're really police officers?" she said. "Why do you want to keep me here? Why won't you tell me what's happened to Jeffrey? It's something terrible; I know it is."

Inspector Browning glanced at his partner. Almost imperceptibly Steven Callahan nodded. The inspector picked up the telephone receiver and held it out to Megan. "I suggest you call Scotland Yard, Mrs. Brookfield. If you don't know the number, ask the operator. That way, you'll be sure you're really connected to police headquarters. Identify yourself by name and ask to speak to the Special Branch duty officer. Ask him if the department sent anybody to your home today."

Slowly Megan stretched out her hand and took the phone. She asked the operator to connect her with Scotland Yard. Her lips were so stiff that she could hardly repeat her name when she was connected to the Special Branch duty officer. Even over the miles of telephone cable she could hear the heightened interest of the policeman as soon as she identified herself.

"Mrs. Brookfield?" he said. "Where are you calling from?"

"From Cambridge."

"From your home?"

"Yes. How did you know I live here?"

"Your address was included in the briefing notice, Mrs. Brookfield. What can I do for you? Is there some problem?"

You could tell me why my name is so familiar at London's police headquarters, she wanted to say. You could tell me what's happened to Jeffrey. Or what Jeffrey's done besides commit bigamy. She pushed that unwelcome thought away. "There are two men at my cottage," she said quickly, although she no longer doubted that the men were government employees. "Were they sent here by your department?"

"Inspector Sidney Browning of the Special Branch drove to Cambridge this morning," said the policeman. "I believe he was assigned a partner who flew in from the United States a couple of days ago, a senior operative from the Central Intelligence Agency."

"I see," she said, although in fact she understood nothing at all. "Could you tell me why an American agent was sent to help out the British police?"

"I have nothing to do with the case, Mrs. Brookfield, but I suppose he was assigned because you are an American citizen. There may be other reasons."

"Because *I'm* an American . . . ?" She closed her eyes for a moment, trying to make sense of the man's answer, but there was no way to give his words meaning. "Thank you for the information," she said and hung up the phone.

She waited for a moment before turning to face the two silent officers. "Okay," she said. "Scotland Yard's Special Branch confirms that you're here legally. But would you *please* stop all this fencing and tell me what's going on? I have a right to know, and if you won't tell me, I'm going to call my lawyer."

Steven Callahan glanced at his watch. "If I remember correctly, it's only a few moments until newstime," he said. "Let's turn on the TV and see how much of your husband's life story they've been able to string together in the past half-hour. The government was scheduled to make its first announcement at nine o'clock."

She supposed she ought to have felt some degree of

shock at his words, but her system was no longer capable of registering emotion. She turned obediently and stared at the flickering screen, scarcely noticing when Inspector Browning leaned over and turned up the sound.

The familiar features of the morning newscaster smiled out into Megan's living room. After a cheerful greeting, his professional smile faded, to be replaced by the solemn expression normally reserved for the transmission of bad news. The lead story, Megan concluded, was either a disastrous rise in unemployment figures or a major plane crash. She quickly discovered that it was neither.

"Tass, the official news agency of the Soviet Union, today announced the arrival in Moscow of British physicist, Dr. Jeffrey Brookfield. Dr. Brookfield, they claim, has asked the Soviet government for political asylum so that he can, quote, 'pursue his experiments in a nation dedicated to the pursuit of world peace and freedom for all workers.' End quote.

"Dr. Brookfield was engaged in research on the creation of controlled release of energy by means of nuclear fusion. He was working closely with scientists at Princeton University in the United States, where the first successful fusion of hydrogen nuclei recently took place.

"So far the British government has neither confirmed nor denied the reports of the Soviet news agency."

The camera angle changed, and the newsman paused slightly before continuing. "A spokesman at the British Foreign Office today denied that Dr. Brookfield's defection reinforced recent worries about deficiencies in British counterintelligence. Dr. Brookfield's wife, an American citizen, is being held in protective custody..."

The announcer was still speaking, but Megan could restrain herself no longer. She thrust one hand in front of her mouth and clutched her other hand around her stomach. She made it to the upstairs bathroom just before she was violently, desperately sick.

Chapter Two

WHEN SHE CAME out of the bathroom, she found Steven Callahan waiting in the tiny upstairs corridor, slouched against the wall in studied indolence. He had discarded his raincoat, and she saw that he was dressed in an informal light gray suit and a white shirt. His hands were thrust into his pants pockets.

Only his eyes betrayed the falseness of his casual pose. They scrutinized Megan with a piercing, brilliant intensity that brought a rush of heat into her cheeks. She had planned to go into the bedroom and change her clothes, but for some reason she found herself unable to move away. She froze outside the bathroom door, her palms pressed flat against its wooden panels.

"You were in there a long time," he said finally. "Are you all right?"

There wasn't a trace of warmth in the question, and she replied with equal coldness. "Yes, thank you. It... the news... was a shock, that's all."

"Was it, Mrs. Brookfield?"

The ironic tone of his question was unmistakable, and the reason for the presence of the two security agents struck Megan with sudden, blinding force. "Oh, my God!" she breathed. "You think I knew what Jeffrey was planning to do. You think I helped him escape!"

"'Escape' is an interesting choice of words, Mrs. Brookfield. England isn't a prison. On the contrary, it's one of the most open societies in the world. Law-abiding citizens are entitled to enter and leave the country whenever they want to."

"I didn't mean what you're implying..."

"I'm implying nothing, Mrs. Brookfield. Are you ready to come downstairs and answer a few questions now, or would you care to rest for a minute or two?"

The careful courtesy of his words brought home the reality of her predicament as almost nothing else could have done. He was talking to her the way detectives always talk to criminal suspects, she thought. She had seen just that sort of determined politeness in a hundred different movies. She'd even seen it in real policemen, when the television news showed the arrest of some vile mass murderer or gangland narcotics dealer.

Just for a moment the mind-wrenching absurdity of her situation threatened her with a fresh spasm of nausea, but she swallowed hard and forced her hands to release their convulsive grip on the comforting ridges of the door.

"I'm not ready to answer your questions yet," she

said, keeping her eyes averted. "I want to change my clothes."

"Go ahead. I'll be waiting outside your bedroom."

She managed not to display any alarm at the warning implicit in his words. She walked past him quickly, taking care to avoid touching him in the narrow confines of the corridor. She was just entering her bedroom when the silence of the cottage was broken by the loud ring of the doorbell.

She whirled round, her heart leaping into her throat. Her nervousness at such an everyday sound made her realize how shattered her nerves were. "Who's that? What do they want?"

"I don't know. May I come into your room?" He followed her into the bedroom without waiting for a response, crossing to the window and pulling aside the filmy lace curtain. "Reporters," he said succinctly. "Two television minicam crews. I'm only surprised nobody got here sooner. The wire services and the daily newspapers will have their people here any minute, you know."

Megan sank onto the bed. "What do they want? Why are they all here?"

"I guess they want to talk to you."

"Oh, no, I can't talk to them! What could I possibly say? Please, Mr. Callahan, you won't make me talk to them, will you?"

He looked at her briefly, his gaze not quite as hard as it had been before, and she glimpsed a curious flicker of emotion in the dark blue depths of his eyes. It was gone almost as soon as she saw it. "You don't have to talk to any reporters if you don't want to. In fact, we'd rather you stayed away from them. Don't worry, Inspector Browning will take care of it."

Even as he spoke, the inspector appeared in the doorway. He nodded toward Megan. "Feeling better, Mrs. Brookfield? Impatient-sounding lot, aren't they? Put a television camera in a man's hands, and he thinks he's got the right to go anywhere. I'll deal with them, Steve, if you like."

"Thanks. There's no need to depart from the statement we agreed on during the drive, is there?"

"No. Don't worry; they'll get nothing exciting out of me. I'm a veteran stonewaller." The endless ringing of the bell was joined by the loud and repeated banging of the door knocker.

"Good Lord, just listen to that racket. I'd better get a move on." With surprising agility for such a stolid-looking man, Inspector Browning hurried down the narrow wooden stairs to the front door.

Megan jumped up from the bed, twisting her fingers tightly together. "He won't let them . . . They won't come in, will they?"

"No. As you heard, we've already prepared a statement, and the inspector will make it clear that there will be no interviews with you."

"Will they go away once he's spoken to them?"

"You know better than that, Mrs. Brookfield. However, a uniformed policeman should arrive within the next half-hour, and he'll do his best to encourage the reporters to disperse. Of course, they'll sound out your neighbors to see if they can come up with any juicy gossip about you and your husband."

"We . . . I hardly know our neighbors. I've only been living here a couple of months."

Callahan's voice was very dry. "I doubt if that will stop the neighbors from coming up with some fascinating stories about you both. I guarantee that at least one person on this street will inform anybody who asks him that he's known for months that the pair of you were up to no good."

The babble of voices at the front door suddenly increased in volume. Megan could hear the shouted questions of the reporters and the inspector's brief, unemotional replies. Feeling as if she were penned inside a cage, she walked toward the window, thinking that by actually seeing what was happening she could lessen the impact of the disembodied shouts and growls. Callahan reached out and grabbed her wrist as she passed him, pulling her to him.

For the second or so that he held her, his fingers felt cool, hard, and as binding as handcuffs. He dropped her wrist almost as quickly as he'd seized it, leaving behind a faint ache. "Keep away from the window unless you want to see yourself on the evening news," he said curtly. "The minicams have telescopic lenses, and there aren't that many windows in this cottage for them to keep covered."

His terse warning was the final misery in a world already turned upside down. Megan felt a wave of giddiness approaching, and she reached out to clutch at a nearby chair. The flowers of the bedroom wallpaper slowly blurred into a solid cream and pink glow. The next thing she knew, she was sitting on the bed with her head between her knees and Callahan's muscular arm around her shoulders, forcing her down.

"I'm all right now," she said as soon as she could speak.

He immediately got up from the bed. "Have you eaten today, Mrs. Brookfield?"

"No. I wasn't very hungry this morning. I told you, I had a headache."

She waited, bracing herself for another of his mocking remarks, but it didn't come. He walked to the bedroom door and cautiously opened it.

"Inspector Browning has shut the front door behind him, so it's safe to go down to the kitchen. I suggest you make yourself some breakfast, Mrs. Brookfield. You'll feel better after you've eaten."

She had no desire to eat anything, but she also lacked the energy to argue. "Perhaps you're right," she said meekly.

He stood to one side, gesturing to indicate that she should precede him down the stairs. Once in the kitchen, she put two slices of bread into the toaster and reached for the percolator in an almost reflexive movement. "Would you like a cup?" she asked, measuring ground beans into the basket.

"Thank you. It would be very welcome."

He refused her offer of toast, and she sat at the kitchen table forcing herself to eat. Callahan was apparently preoccupied with drinking his coffee, but Megan knew, with a certainty she didn't attempt to analyze, that his attention was riveted on her slightest movement.

More to break his concentrated scrutiny than for any other reason she made the effort to speak to him. "Why are you here, Mr. Callahan?" she asked quietly. "Why has the American government sent a CIA field operative to question the wife of a British...of a British..."

"Defector?" he supplied.

She forced herself to speak the word. "Yes. A British defector."

"You're an American citizen."

"But *I* haven't defected." She raised her chin defiantly. "Nor do I intend to defect, Mr. Callahan."

His gaze was cool, impersonal, as it flicked over her. "You'll have no chance to do so while I'm here. It's my job to see that you don't join your husband."

"And *that's* why the American government sent you?"

There was the tiniest of pauses before he spoke again. "Not entirely. Your husband was working in close cooperation with scientists at Princeton University. The United States government has a legitimate interest in knowing precisely how much classified data Dr. Brookfield has taken with him."

Megan closed her eyes, trying to reject the image of Jeffrey as a betrayer of his university colleagues and a traitor to his country. Two months earlier, before their supposed wedding ceremony, she would have vehemently denied the possibility that mild, earnest, modest Jeffrey could be a traitor. After two months of living with him, she was no longer so sure.

She opened her eyes, not wanting Callahan to see how troubled she was. Even as she glanced up, the inspector walked into the room. "I've pacified that lot for a few minutes," he said. "And the squad car has arrived. The local police have sent two uniformed officers. We've put one out at the front of the house and the other at the back, so you're quite safe for now. No reporters are going to get past the garden gates while they're on duty."

"Thank you." Megan saw that he was trying to be kind, and she was genuinely grateful. It was an effort, but from somewhere she managed to drag out a smile.

Callahan returned his cup to the kitchen table with a distinct thump. "We still have questions to ask you, Mrs. Brookfield. Do you want to stay here, or would you prefer to go into the living room?"

"It doesn't matter."

"The living room I think," the inspector said cheerily. "There are armchairs in there, and we may as well be comfortable."

"Give me three minutes, and I'll set it up," Callahan said, leaving the room without waiting to hear the inspector's agreement.

"We'll clear away the breakfast things while we're waiting, shall we?" The inspector carried the dirty cups to the sink and ran hot water over them, adding a squirt of detergent from the plastic bottle under the sink. The ridiculous, cozy domesticity of the scene renewed Megan's sense of unreality, and she had to stuff her hand against her mouth to prevent a gasp of laughter from escaping.

The inspector stacked the cups on the draining rack, seemingly unaware of her tension. "There," he said, as he dried his hands. "Steve should be ready for us by now."

Her feeling of taking part in some black comedy disappeared abruptly when they entered the living room. Callahan had drawn the heavy velvet drapes, shutting out the watery morning sun. He had switched on all the lights, and the room looked forbidding in the harsh electric brilliance.

"Why have you closed the drapes?" she asked. A tiny spurt of anger pierced the numbing effect of her fear.

"The reporters are still outside, Mrs. Brookfield, and this room is clearly visible from the road. I thought you would prefer some privacy. I had no sinister motive, I assure you."

She sat on the sofa, deliberately angling her body so

that she was in no danger of finding her eyes suddenly in contact with his. "What sort of things do you want to ask me?" she asked stiffly, directing her attention to Inspector Browning.

"Just a few routine questions," he replied. From the corner of her eye she saw Callahan lean over, and then she heard the distinct click of a recorder being switched on. She jumped up.

"What are you doing?"

Callahan's voice and gaze remained level. "It's in your interest as well as ours to have an accurate record of this interview, Mrs. Brookfield."

"But I haven't done anything, and you're treating me like a criminal!"

"We've simply asked you to help us check on some information. As far as I'm aware, nobody has even hinted that you might be guilty of any infringement of the law. However, you can call a lawyer if you want to."

She walked over to the window, longing to throw back the drapes and let in some sunshine, but she discovered that Callahan was right: she wasn't willing to expose herself to the tender mercies of the press photographers. "Can my lawyer keep you from questioning me?"

"No, not in general terms. In certain circumstances he can advise you not to answer specific questions."

"I guess you may as well ask whatever you want to know," she said wearily. "The sooner I've given you the information you need, the sooner you'll leave me in peace."

"We appreciate your cooperation." The inspector smiled approvingly. "How long have you been in England, Mrs. Brookfield?"

"Two years."

"Why did you come here?"

"I'm a trained archivist, and I was offered the opportunity to work in Cambridge University as part of my doctoral program. Naturally, I jumped at the chance."

"Your family didn't object to you traveling so far away from home?" Steve Callahan asked.

The pause before she answered was so slight that she hoped he might not notice it. "I was twenty-five years old when I left Washington. I'd been independent of my family for some time."

"Has your family met Dr. Brookfield? Did they come over for your wedding?"

"No." She walked back to the sofa with quick, jerky steps. "Why do you have to ask me all these questions? They have nothing to do with what happened to Jeffrey. Your departments must know how long I've been in Cambridge. Immigration officials keep a record on all aliens entering the country."

"Yes, that's true," Callahan said. "But your cooperation will save our computer staff a great deal of time in checking through the records. And, of course, I'm sure you're anxious to see that the correct version of all the facts goes down in our official report. Just for the record, Mrs. Brookfield, how did you meet your husband?"

"We met at a party four months ago."

"And how long have you been married?"

She stared down at her hands. Was this the moment to tell them? If she admitted that she had never been legally married to Jeffrey, that the ceremony they had gone through was meaningless because he already had a wife, would they leave her alone? Or would it merely mean a fresh round of even more painful questions, and even more scandalous publicity in the muckraking press?

"Mrs. Brookfield?" Callahan's cold voice broke into her tumultuous thoughts before she could make up her mind what to say. "I asked how long you've been married to Dr. Brookfield."

"Two months," she said, not knowing she would keep up the lie until she had actually spoken. "We were married on the first of April." April Fools' Day, she thought wryly. Maybe Jeffrey had a sense of humor after all.

"Could you give me a list of the friends you've spent the most time with since your marriage? Particularly any new ones who were originally friends of your husband."

"Dr. Andrew Vitoll, the head of the library where I work, came to dinner last month, and one of Jeffrey's colleagues from the university lab joined us. Her name is Helen Meaney. I believe she was Jeffrey's personal assistant."

"And who else, Mrs. Brookfield?" Callahan prompted, when it became apparent that she didn't plan to add anything more.

She suddenly felt a huge impatience with all the half-truths and lies she had told over the past two months in an effort to save her own pride. Why couldn't she tell the truth and admit that Jeffrey had scarcely ever spent an evening at home with her, let alone encouraged her to meet his friends? There was no longer any point in pretending that everything about their marriage had been perfect, when obviously everything about it had been all wrong. Perhaps, after all, she didn't have to blame herself for the failure of their relationship. It was rapidly becoming apparent that Jeffrey had set out to deceive her from the night of their very first date.

"As a matter of fact, I hardly met any of Jeffrey's friends," she said. "We didn't spend many evenings together because he worked late almost every night. I guess, in view of what's happened, it would be reasonable to conclude that he didn't want me to meet his colleagues."

"So you're suggesting that you don't know much about your husband's friends and activities, Mrs. Brookfield?"

"No, I'm not suggesting that, Mr. Callahan. I'm stating it as a fact. In two months of marriage Jeffrey and I spent no more than five evenings together."

Callahan's expression became skeptical. "An unusual situation for a newly married couple, wouldn't you say, Mrs. Brookfield?"

"I have no idea. Maybe." With a further spurt of defiance she looked directly at him. "This is the first time I've been married. I don't claim to be an expert on typical newlywed behavior."

"Quite so," the inspector intervened smoothly. "And what about relatives, Mrs. Brookfield. Did you meet any of your husband's family?"

"Jeffrey was an only child. His parents are dead."

"And you, Mrs. Brookfield? Are you an only child?"

"No," she said. "I have eight brothers and sisters."

She heard the faint exclamation, quickly smothered, that came from Callahan's corner of the room, and she knew that she had finally succeeded in surprising him. "Nine children in the family!" he exclaimed, and for a moment his eyes crinkled with a hint of humor. "That's quite a collection!"

"Yes."

He grinned again, more openly, and she noticed irrelevantly that his entire face was altered when he smiled.

Even the blue of his eyes became less piercing, darkening with warmth. "It's unusual to encounter such a large family nowadays," he said. "Whereabouts do you fit, Mrs. Brookfield? Oldest? Youngest? In the middle?"

"I'm the oldest," she said. Some demon, some childish desire to shock that she couldn't understand, compelled her to add, "I don't want you to get the wrong idea, Mr. Callahan. I'm not the oldest daughter in a big, old-fashioned happy family. My parents married each other in college, and I arrived six months later. My father has been married twice more since then, and when I left the States, my mother was in the process of divorcing her fourth husband. Knowing my mother, I would imagine she's working on her next marital prospect by now, unless she's already married him. My three half brothers and five half sisters are products of five different marriages, and I've given up counting how many stepbrothers and stepsisters have flitted in and out of my life. I certainly can't remember all of their names or even which child belonged to which stepfather. From third grade until my sophomore year in high school, my mother changed her place of residence approximately every year."

"Place of residence?" Callahan murmured on a note of inquiry.

"An accurate description, Mr. Callahan, not a slip of the tongue. My mother isn't the sort of woman who creates a home."

"I see," he said, and she was suddenly afraid that he did, indeed, see a great deal of the hurt and loneliness she usually struggled to keep hidden. The more she thought about it, the less she understood why she had chosen to confide the truth about her rootless, erratic childhood.

The police were suspicious enough of her motives already. She didn't need to give them grounds to think she was emotionally unstable.

"What happened in your sophomore year?" Callahan asked. "You indicated that you stopped moving."

She perched on the padded arm of the sofa, not looking at him but trying to appear at ease. "My father had just married for the third time. I went to live with him and his new wife. They let me stay long enough to graduate from high school and get accepted into college. Actually, my father finally seems to have found the magic formula for marital bliss. He and Lorraine, his third wife, have stayed together for eleven years."

"Practice makes perfect," Callahan murmured with a faint grin that disappeared almost before she was sure she had seen it. To her relief, he changed the subject without asking any more questions about her relationship with her parents. "Mrs. Brookfield, could you describe your husband for me?"

"He's nearly six feet tall, thin, brown hair..."

"No, I didn't mean his physical appearance. We have photographs. What is he like as a man? As a husband?"

"Jeffrey is... was..." She drew another breath and tried again. "Jeffrey appeared to be calm, stable, methodical, and extremely reliable," she said curtly.

"And that's why you married him, because he seemed so reliable?"

She sprang off the arm of the sofa. "Yes, Mr. Callahan, that's exactly why I married Jeffrey. Because he was stolid and secure and *safe*—all the things that were missing from my childhood. You see, I'm perfectly capable of psychoanalyzing my need for security. You don't have to do it for me." She couldn't quite manage to control the lump that pushed its way up into her throat, thickening her voice. "Since I can do such a great job of self-analysis, it's a pity I did such a lousy job of judging Jeffrey's character, isn't it?"

Her outburst was followed by a moment of silence that was eventually interrupted by the loud ringing of the phone.

"I'll take the call in the kitchen," Inspector Browning said, hurrying from the room.

The door closed behind the inspector, and she looked in Callahan's direction, not attempting to conceal her irritation. "He seems very confident the call's for him."

"Yes. It won't be for you." There was another pause. "There's been a tap on your phone for some time. And somebody from the Special Branch has been assigned to intercept all incoming calls since yesterday evening. That's why the press and the TV stations weren't able to reach you by phone."

She felt the blood drain out of her cheeks, leaving her white and shaking with anger. "How dare they! It's illegal to tap people's phones!"

"Not in cases involving national security, Mrs. Brookfield. The laws in the United States and in the United Kingdom are quite similar in that regard. If enough evidence can be produced to justify reasonable suspicion, a wiretap can be introduced." He turned and stared into the empty fire grate. "Dr. Brookfield has been under surveillance by MI 6 for the last five months, I believe. Governments nowadays go to great lengths to keep new commercial techniques from falling into the wrong hands."

"You mean Jeffrey was being watched before he even met me?" Megan's brain was too cluttered and too bewildered to work out precisely why, but she felt sure the question was a significant one.

"Yes." Callahan gave up his apparent fascination with the empty fireplace and turned around to look at her. "Do you by any chance keep liquor in that corner cabinet, Mrs. Brookfield? You look a bit pale. Can I get you a drink?" When she didn't immediately respond, he hesitated for a moment, then repeated, "Mrs. Brookfield?"

She whirled around, knowing that her nerves were stretched tauter than a set of guitar strings and hating the fact that she might at any moment burst into tears. "For heaven's sake stop calling me Mrs. Brookfield every time you open your mouth!" she snapped. "It isn't even my real name!"

Chapter Three

HE STOOD PERFECTLY still as the grandfather clock in the corner of the room ticked off the endless seconds. She could see only his back, and when at last he turned to face her, his expression was guarded, his eyes carefully blank.

"I don't understand what you mean, Mrs. Brook—" He cut off the word abruptly. "I think you'd better explain exactly what you mean."

Megan walked as far away from him as she could in the small room. She bitterly regretted the crazy impulse that had caused her to blurt out the truth. She couldn't understand why the mere presence of Callahan seemed to set her so much on edge. There was no reason why she should trust him to keep personal information confidential. She might not know much about the strange world of international intrigue, but she knew enough to be quite sure that when a major defection occurred, publicity of the right sort—on both sides—was the name of the game.

Megan twisted her fingers into a tight knot as she thought of the press reports that would inevitably appear, both in England and in the States. As clearly as if they were standing next to each other, she could visualize her mother's faintly malicious smile when she read the news that her prim and proper daughter had been living with the notorious traitor in a bigamous marriage. She could almost hear her mother's voice dripping with false sympathy as she carefully chose the words most calculated to cut and wound a daughter she had never wanted and always disliked.

"I'm still waiting for your explanation," Callahan said softly, a hint of steel under the quiet words.

Megan couldn't look at him. "I didn't mean anything particularly significant. I guess I'm just tired of British formality, the way everybody here always calls you by your surname, even when they've known you for years and years. You're American. You know things are different in the States."

"And you're an intelligent woman, so I know you don't expect me to believe that explanation. Why don't you save us both time and tell me what you really meant?"

The inspector poked his head around the door. "Steve, come into the kitchen for a moment, please. There's something you have to discuss with your headquarters."

"I'll be right there." Callahan's gaze narrowed as he looked at Megan. "I'll be interested in continuing our conversation as soon as I return, *Mrs. Brookfield*. Wait for me here, please."

She expected Inspector Browning to remain in the living room, but he simply nodded to her politely and followed Callahan into the kitchen. She could hear nothing except the faint murmur of their voices through the thick walls of the old cottage, and for a few seconds she was content to luxuriate in the momentary reprieve from questioning. But almost immediately the brief feeling of relaxation passed. Callahan would come back, she knew, and when he did, the relentless questions about her marriage would start again.

She paced restlessly around the room, finally walking over to the window and peering through a minute opening in the drapes. Her front gate was surrounded by people, and a uniformed policeman was guarding the entrance to the tiny front garden. The reporters all seemed to be chatting together in a desultory and good-natured fashion. It was an eerie sensation to see so many people clustered on the pavement outside her home, knowing they were all waiting for the sole purpose of interviewing her. After she had watched them for a minute or so, however, the eeriness passed, and the watchful presence of the press no longer seemed as threatening as it had been an hour earlier. She recognized Robert Heath, chief interviewer for the BBC news, and she began to wonder if she ought to take this opportunity to give him her side of the story. In comparison to what Callahan had in store for her, persistent reporters began to seem no more than a mild annoyance.

She dropped the drape back into place and hurried out of the living room. She ran quietly into the hallway, her heart thudding as she opened the hall closet and pulled out the first jacket that came to hand. She thrust her arms into it, reaching up at the same time to take her shoulder bag down from the closet shelf. It took less than a minute to creep across the final few feet of hallway and wrench open the front door.

She slammed it triumphantly behind her, not caring if she made a noise. The journalists would automatically provide her with protection. Neither Callahan nor the inspector would be prepared to drag her forcibly back inside the house with television cameras recording their every move. In retrospect, she couldn't imagine why she hadn't thought earlier of using the crush of reporters as a means of escape. She had credit cards with her. She would simply hole up somewhere and refuse to answer any more questions. She was sure such a move would be entirely within her legal rights.

As soon as she completed the short walk down the garden path, she realized that her plan had been a mistake. The police constable, who was concentrating on keeping the reporters outside the gate, was not aware of her arrival until she slipped out onto the narrow sidewalk and stood next to him. So far, so good, but a solid wall of bodies prevented her from moving any farther. Robert Heath was the first reporter to approach her. He quickly threw away the cigarette he had been smoking and pushed his way around the police constable. He held a mike over the heads of his rivals and called out to her. "Will you be joining your husband in Moscow, Mrs. Brookfield?"

"No!"

She had no opportunity to say anything more. Her answer was a signal for the other reporters to thrust their mikes forward as they yelled out a wild cacophony of questions. Flashbulbs exploded, and the television camera crews moved into action, but there was nowhere for her to hide.

"When did you find out your husband was leaving?"

"Did you know Dr. Brookfield was a Communist?"

"Is it true your husband was blackmailed into cooperating with the Soviets, Mrs. Brookfield?"

"Is it true you were a member of Communist Youth International when you were a student in the United States?"

"No!" she cried out, horrified at the distortions already gaining currency among the reporters. "The most radical student group I belonged to was one trying to stop the slaughter of baby seals!"

The questions started again immediately, but she was unable to assimilate more than a tenth of them, and equally unable to make her answers heard above the din of voices. She tried to push through the reporters into the main street, but it was like pushing against a steel retaining wall.

She turned around and found she couldn't even return to the relative sanctuary of her front garden. The policeman, sweating profusely beneath his helmet, was struggling to keep the gate locked, barring the way with one hand while at the same time calling an urgent message for assistance into a two-way radio that he held in the other. In the crush of bodies, there was no way to swing the iron gate open.

Because of the direction in which she was facing, she probably saw the flashing blue lights of the police squad car before anybody else. It rounded the corner from the rear of her house at considerable speed and drew to a halt at the curb directly opposite her. With a sigh of relief, which she didn't stop to analyze in the heat of the moment, she saw Callahan spring out of the car and push his way toward her.

His arm clamped around her shoulders, pulling her firmly against the iron-hard solidity of his chest. Instinctively, she allowed her body to yield to his strength.

"Oh, Callahan," she murmured. "Get me out of here. Please."

His arms tightened fractionally. "Mrs. Brookfield has no further statements to make at this time." His voice cut through a fresh wave of questions. "Excuse me," he said to the reporters closest to him. "We're leaving."

He didn't wait to hear their response. Using his shoulder to clear a path, his arms still wrapped reassuringly around Megan, he forced his way to the curb. The back door of the squad car was open, its engine running. "Get in," he said, bundling her into the car. As soon as he joined her inside, the car roared away. He leaned forward, pulling the door closed as they rounded the corner at the end of the street.

The silence in the car was broken only by the purr of the engine and the crackle of static on the two-way radio. Megan hunched herself into the corner of the rear seat, as far away from Callahan as she could get. She straightened her clothes and tucked her hair behind her ears, mortified at the way she had behaved. She recognized Inspector Browning's sturdy shoulders bent over the steering wheel, but she couldn't see his face. She could see Callahan's, however, and his expression wasn't encouraging. Whatever had possessed her? Why had she clung to him like that, burying her face in his jacket as if she couldn't bear to let him go?

He turned to look at her, and she felt the color blaze

in her cheeks. "Thank you for getting me out of there," she said, when the silence threatened to become unendurable. "I was scared. Now I understand what it must feel like to be president or a member of the royal family. I don't know how they stand that sort of pressure for years on end."

"They exercise a great deal of self-discipline, I imagine," Callahan replied coolly. Almost without pause, he added, "We asked you to remain in the living room, Mrs. Brookfield."

She heard the faint emphasis on her surname and felt her cheeks flame with even brighter color. The memory of the way she had collapsed into his arms, murmuring his name, was disconcertingly vivid, and she tried to conceal her embarrassment with anger. "You had no right to keep me a virtual prisoner in my own home. I've done nothing, nothing at all to deserve it!"

She sensed his hesitation. "We have some more questions to ask you," he said finally, but she was convinced that the relatively mild statement wasn't what he had originally planned to say.

Inspector Browning broke into the conversation. "I think we've managed to avoid any overeager pursuers," he said. "Fortunately, the police constable was smart enough to force the reporters to park their cars quite a way from the cottage. It's amazing how even the most determined news hound comes unglued at the thought of having his car towed away by the police department."

Steve Callahan leaned back in his seat, the severity of his expression fading slightly. "Look up ahead, Sidney. If you're sure we've shaken them, that looks like a good place to make a stop."

"Yes, all right. I'll pull over."

The car drew to a smooth halt, and Megan felt her stomach knot with apprehension. She bit back a nervous bubble of laughter when she realized why they had stopped. The detectives, it seemed, were intent on nothing more menacing than picking up some fried chicken. She glanced at her watch and saw that it was considerably past lunchtime. At the same moment, she became aware that she was ravenously hungry.

In less than five minutes Callahan returned to the car, carrying a large striped container. Megan's mouth began to water. "It's too damp for a picnic, even if we knew somewhere inconspicuous to go," he said. "I hope you can find the way back to the cottage, Sidney, because I haven't the faintest idea how to get there."

"No problem. I'll go round a couple of side streets, and we'll approach the cottage from the back. With any luck we'll be able to get in unobserved. They won't be expecting us to return so soon, I shouldn't think."

A brief exchange on the radio confirmed that the rear entrance to the cottage was deserted except for the second police constable and a few curious passersby. In fact, the policeman added, the crowd of reporters at the front had thinned considerably since Mrs. Brookfield left the house.

"I'll bet!" the inspector said, signing off. "We'll see you in a couple of minutes, Bob."

"Why have some of the reporters gone?" Megan asked. "Why aren't you surprised?"

Callahan's smile was grim. "It means that with one brief appearance you've provided them with more than enough copy to fill their time slots or their column inches. A couple of shots of the beautiful, deserted wife, followed by some dramatic footage as she's hustled into the police squad car. That's dynamite news coverage. You may as well face up to the fact that the media will have a field day with this. You make very good-looking copy, Mrs. Brookfield."

She was saved the necessity of answering, because at that moment they arrived at the back entrance to the cottage. A young police constable politely opened the car door for her, and Megan thanked him before hurrying up the short path to the kitchen door. She didn't want to risk another encounter with the reporters.

She was reaching into her purse when Callahan said, "I have the key for this door, Mrs. Brookfield. Would you stand aside while I open it?"

The inspector followed them into the warm kitchen, bolting the outer door behind him. "Well, now, this is going to be very pleasant. If you'll excuse me, Mrs. Brookfield, I'll just wash my hands while you and Steve divide up the goodies."

As soon as he left the room, Megan walked to the sink, hanging her jacket and purse on the hook beside the back door. She washed and dried her hands, then selected three pottery plates from the cupboard next to the sink.

"Do you want to wash up, too?" she asked, not looking at Callahan. "There's a little bathroom at the end of the hallway."

"I can wash my hands here," he answered. "Why don't you divide the chicken? There are some french fries in the carton as well."

"Chips," she murmured unthinkingly.

"I beg your pardon?"

"They're called chips here," she said. "Not french fries. And potato chips are called crisps."

"I appreciate the lesson," he said dryly. "Could you please serve the chicken and... chips?"

The inspector returned just as she finished putting the paper napkins next to each plate. He smiled genially before pulling a stool up to the small kitchen table. "Now this is very nice indeed, very cozy. You've no idea, Mrs. Brookfield, how much we old-timers appreciate the fact that American fast food has arrived on this side of the Atlantic."

Megan returned his smile, but allowed her astonishment to show. "From the newspaper articles I've read, I had the impression that most people in Britain thought that hamburgers and fried chicken were only one step up from synthesized cardboard."

"Ah, you can't believe everything you read in the newspapers." The inspector was apparently unaware of any possible double meaning to his statement. He took a generous bite out of a crunchy drumstick and chewed contentedly. "If you pay attention to the papers, you'd think these franchise operations had caused the ruination of the best eating places in Europe. But if you talk to an old policeman like me, or to a traveling salesman, or to anybody who's on the road a lot, you'll realize that what's gone wasn't half as good or a tenth as clean as these new hamburger places."

"Have you offered your advertising services to the American embassy?" Callahan asked with a hint of a smile. "They'd have one of your quotes in a brochure before you could turn around."

"I'll bear it in mind." The inspector carefully wiped his fingers on his napkin, giving a slight sigh. "Now a good English beer would make that a perfect meal."

Megan jumped up. "I'm sorry, I didn't think to offer

you anything to drink. I believe Jeffrey left some beer in the back of the refrigerator..." Her voice died as the inspector straightened in his chair.

"That's very kind of you, but I won't have a beer just now. Puts me to sleep if I indulge at lunchtime."

"It wouldn't have anything to do with the fact that you're not allowed to drink on duty, would it?" she asked with an unintentional touch of bitterness.

"That, too," he said, his cheerful expression unruffled. "Could I put the kettle on for a cup of tea, if it wouldn't be troubling you too much, Mrs. Brookfield?"

"Please do." She got up and put a caddy of loose tea on the counter together with a brown earthenware teapot. "Perhaps you should make it as well. Jeffrey was always telling me I had no idea how to make a decent cup of English tea."

"Was he?" the inspector said, turning on the gas under the kettle. "I heard that in the States most people drink their tea without milk. Sounds very strange to us over here, that does."

Steven Callahan pushed back his stool with considerable force. His eyes were hard as he turned to face Megan. "I think it's time to cut out the social chitchat. I'd like to know why you said earlier that Brookfield was not, and I quote, your 'real name.'"

At his curt words, the atmosphere in the kitchen underwent an immediate change. The inspector stopped puttering with the teapot, and Steve Callahan continued to stare at Megan with relentless, implacable determination. She floundered for a moment, wondering what to say. In the end it seemed simplest to tell the truth.

"Jeffrey and I weren't married."

For a split second Steve Callahan's face was wiped

clean of all expression. Then his eyes narrowed. "I've seen a copy of your marriage certificate, Mrs. Brookfield. It was in the briefing file prepared for me by my counterpart in British government service."

"Maybe you have. The certificate doesn't mean anything. Jeffrey already had another wife when he married me."

The kettle whistled into the sudden silence. The inspector turned off the heat and added boiling water to the teapot before saying, "I want to get this quite clear. You mean Dr. Brookfield had a legal wife, not an ex-wife or a mistress?"

"Yes, inspector, that's exactly what I mean. Jeffrey had a legal wife."

"What's her name, and where does she live?" Steve Callahan asked brusquely. "Did you know of her existence when you agreed to go through a wedding ceremony with Dr. Brookfield?"

"Of course not! And I don't know her name. I don't know anything about her." Wearily Megan rubbed a hand across her eyes. "I only found out about her the day Jeffrey left. He was packing the last of his suitcases when he said I ought to forget about our marriage, because it had never been real. He had another wife, a woman he'd been married to for years, and so I wouldn't even have to get a divorce, because our marriage wasn't legal. It had never existed except in my mind."

The confession was so humiliating that she took care to avoid looking at either of the men. She felt the light touch of Steve's hand on her shoulders with a faint start of surprise, but she allowed him to lead her back to the table. He gently pushed her down into a chair, and the inspector put a steaming cup of milky tea in front of her.

Refuge In His Arms

She accepted it gratefully. After two years in England she had almost become accustomed to the strong-brewed flavor mingled with creamy milk. At this precise moment anything that gave her something to do and somewhere to look was welcome.

She was aware of the inspector and Callahan exchanging glances above her head. The inspector finished his tea and placed the empty cup neatly in the sink. "Well, Mrs.—er—"

"I guess I'm not Mrs. anything. My maiden name was Richards."

"Well, then, Miss Richards, you've given us something interesting to work on now, and that's a fact. I'm due back in London before five o'clock so, what with one thing and another, I think I'll be leaving. One of my colleagues will no doubt be driving down to see you in the morning. Steve here will look after you tonight, so you've no need to worry about reporters harassing you or anything like that."

She spoke through stiff lips, her words clipped. "Are you going to tell the reporters I wasn't married to Jeffrey?"

"I wouldn't dream of doing anything so rash." The inspector nodded to Callahan. "Perhaps you'd have a word with me in the living room? I left my raincoat there, I think. Good day to you, Mrs. Brookfield. I enjoyed having lunch with you."

"Wait for me here," Callahan said. "And I mean right *here*."

The two men left the kitchen, and Megan cleared away the remains of lunch with mechanical thoroughness. She hated her surroundings to be messy even though she recognized that her almost obsessive desire for neatness was another hangup from a disordered childhood. By the time she was nine, she had learned that if she wanted to have clean clothes to wear for school she would have to wash them herself. If she wanted to keep a sharpened pencil or a treasured book, she had to hide it from her mother's careless fingers.

The kitchen was once again immaculate, the counters gleaming, the sink scrubbed, when Steve Callahan returned. "The inspector's gone," he said. "Why don't we sit in the other room."

She shrugged, feigning a casualness she didn't feel. "If you like." She had no illusions about his seemingly courteous invitation. It was undoubtedly nerves that caused her pulse to race with a strange tingle of anticipation as she preceded him into the living room.

"This is a pleasant room," he said, relaxing in one of the armchairs. "Did you decorate it yourself?"

"No, Jeffrey lived here for years before I married him. A few of the books are mine. That's all." She forced herself to stop pacing the room and take a seat in the chair opposite him. "Mr. Callahan, what's going to happen now?"

"I think we should relax for a while. Talk a little. See if we can jog your memory about some of Dr. Brookfield's friends."

She sprang up from the chair, abandoning all pretense of calm. "You mean carry on the inquisition, Mr. Callahan? What's the inspector going to do?"

"He's going to coordinate a lot of very boring research work, checking into records, that sort of thing."

"What for? Why does any of that stuff matter? Jeffrey's gone now. There's nothing the British or American government can do to bring him back."

Refuge In His Arms 47

Callahan rose from his chair, his eyes fixed on her with ruthless intensity. Megan trembled with a strange emotion that was not entirely fear. He suddenly seemed overwhelmingly close and the space between them very small.

"If you think about it, Mrs. Brookfield—I mean, Ms. Richards—you'll realize that Dr. Brookfield couldn't have worked alone. The inspector and I plan to make sure that his associates, whoever they may be, don't have any chance to follow him out of the country."

Her hand, which was resting on the low mantelpiece, tightened its grip. "I asked you before not to call me Mrs. Brookfield. My name's Megan."

She was aware once again of a flash of emotion that darkened his eyes, but he said nothing. He merely inclined his head in the briefest of acknowledgments.

"Do you have any idea who Jeffrey's fellow conspirators are?" she asked.

"Naturally the security services have some guesses they're hoping to confirm."

Megan fixed her gaze on the flowered pattern of the rug. "Mr. Callahan, do you think I was helping Jeffrey? Do you think I'm a spy?"

The silence in the room seemed to stretch out forever. His expression didn't change, but she had the distinct impression that she had somehow given him a shock. "I have no official opinion," he said finally, his voice entirely without emotion. "In my job I've learned to avoid making judgments without an adequate factual basis."

"But you must have a personal opinion," she persisted. She looked up aware that she was challenging him by the directness of her gaze. "Why don't you tell me what your really think about me?"

An angry flush darkened his cheekbones. "I think you're too damned attractive for my professional peace of mind," he said tersely. "That's what I think about you... Megan."

Chapter Four

HE TURNED ABRUPTLY, obviously regretting his admission as soon as he'd made it. Megan could see the tension lingering in his powerful, muscular shoulders, and she felt a tiny leap of elation when she realized that she had the power to affect his professional detachment so strongly.

She watched him walk over to the window and half pull back the drapes. A streak of watery afternoon sunshine highlighted the thickness of his blond hair and the coppery tan of his skin. She was disconcerted by the sudden flash of physical awareness that twisted through her. She had always despised people who succumbed to mere sexual attraction. As a teenager she had seen her mother "in love" all too frequently, and she wanted nothing to do with such an irrational, degrading emotion.

Steve drew back the drapes to their fullest extent, then switched off the overhead light. "There are only a couple of reporters left outside," he said. "If we sit away from the windows, I don't think they'll trouble us."

She nodded her agreement, moving her legs slightly when he returned to sit opposite her. She didn't want to feel any part of his body touching hers.

"I apologize for the personal remark I made earlier," he said abruptly. "It was inappropriate." He continued speaking before she could reply. "Are you ready to answer a few more questions about Dr. Brookfield?"

She looked at the deliberate blankness of his expression and began to wonder if she had imagined the flash of raw desire that had darkened his eyes only minutes earlier. She was surprised to discover that she wanted to provoke him again; she wanted to see the man behind the professional mask. She stared fixedly at her hands until her emotions were under their usual rigid control. She didn't like the effect Steve Callahan was having on her.

"Yes, I'm ready," she said finally in a low voice. "You can ask whatever you want."

"Tell me again exactly how you came to marry Jeffrey Brookfield."

She had planned to answer his questions in monosyllables, but suddenly, almost against her will, the words came tumbling out. It was as if explaining things to Steve helped her to make sense of her crazy, unsatisfactory marriage to Jeffrey. The marriage that had turned out not to be a marriage at all, she reminded herself.

"Jeffrey was older than most of the men I'd dated in

the past," she said. "I thought he was the most stable, the most even-tempered person I'd ever met. I was flattered when he seemed so eager to please me. We met at a party late in January, and during the next couple of months we went out to dinner several times. Once or twice we went to the theater or to a concert or an exhibition of student artwork. Jeffrey always seemed calm and polite and sympathetic."

"Is that what you were looking for in a potential husband? Constant calm?"

"No, no of course not." Her denial was a little too vehement, and she added with a touch of wry honesty, "Jeffrey was also a wonderful listener. If you've grown up competing with eight other children for attention, a good listener makes a very attractive date. I guess now I understand why he was so happy to let me talk. If I was busy talking, I was less likely to notice how little he was telling me about himself."

"Didn't you ever discuss his family, even after you married? How about his friends? His hobbies?"

"He said his parents were killed in a car accident on the M1 motorway just as he was about to graduate from the university. He talked about his friends and hobbies only in a general sort of way." She stopped for a moment, remembering the pleasant, uneventful days of their brief courtship. Only after their wedding had Jeffrey set out to turn her dream of happiness into a waking nightmare. "You know, I just realized something," she said. "Before he asked me to marry him, as soon as I expressed an interest in anything, Jeffrey would say he was interested in the same thing. If I mentioned a movie I wanted to see, he would turn up the next day with tickets. Once I said I liked Bach better than Beethoven, and, sure enough, Jeffrey announced that he liked Bach better as well."

Megan twisted a strand of hair nervously around her fingers, then glanced up at Steve. "I was a fool, wasn't I? He was just setting me up so I'd agree to marry him."

For a moment Steve's gaze lingered on her cheeks. "It seems likely," he said.

"Why did Jeffrey go to so much trouble to set me up? Why did he marry me?" She blurted out the questions before she could stop herself, then wished she could call them back. She didn't want Steve to realize how easily Jeffrey had manipulated her need for security.

"Perhaps he fell helplessly in love with you."

Megan's reply held a touch of bitterness. "No," she said. "Believe me, that wasn't the reason."

Steve suddenly stood up and moved restlessly toward the empty fireplace. "How much do you know about Dr. Brookfield's work, Megan?"

"He was working with scientists here in Cambridge and at Princeton University on research into the controlled fusion of hydrogen atoms."

"Do you understand what that means?"

"Not really."

"At the moment nuclear power plants operate on the basis of nuclear fission. The reactors smash atoms apart, producing a lot of radioactive debris in the process. Jeffrey Brookfield was working on nuclear fusion, which is a potentially cheaper and safer form of energy generation. When hydrogen atoms fuse, the reaction produces almost no dangerous radioactive debris, and the raw material cost is low."

"I see. But if his research was so valuable, didn't the

government keep a close eye on what was happening?"

"Of course. When the British government first began to suspect that vital leaks of classified information were occurring, they alerted the American authorities. After a long investigation, both governments decided that the leaks were coming from the Cambridge lab, not from Princeton. Dr. Brookfield was one of a small group of scientists who came under suspicion several months ago. Around Christmas time, in fact."

"Just a few weeks before Jeffrey decided he was interested in me."

Steve Callahan looked at her steadily. "Yes. Precisely that time."

"Why didn't he leave the country if he suspected he was being watched? Why on earth did he waste time dating me?"

Steve shrugged eloquently. "Who knows for sure? His own experiments were at a crucial stage, and the Princeton scientists were on the verge of a major breakthrough. I guess he was desperate to continue at the lab here for another few months. The equipment he was using, you know, cost millions of dollars. The Soviets couldn't duplicate it overnight."

"Then why didn't he simply concentrate on his experiments if he was so pressed for time? Why did he complicate his life by pretending to marry me?"

"Marriage was a very effective ploy. It successfully threw the British security forces off the scent for several weeks. Psychologists have found patterns in the behavior of spies and traitors just before they defect, and people who are planning to cut and run to another country don't usually get married. Divorce, on the other hand, is very common, for some reason."

"I see. Well, Jeffrey managed to fool all of us, didn't he? I guess he was using me right from the moment we first met. He never loved... he never cared for me at all."

"I would think it's likely Dr. Brookfield was using you as a cover," Steve agreed. "But I can't say whether or not he loved you. I have no facts on which to base my judgment."

Megan couldn't control the anger behind her smile. "There speaks the perfect professional investigator. You know something? I've spent most of my life judging situations on the basis of fact, and look where that's landed me. Sometimes I think I might have been better off if I'd just let go of my emotions."

"Maybe." Steve smothered a sudden yawn. His expression was rueful when he met her eyes. "I'm sorry, Megan. I guess I'm too tired for psychological speculation right now."

For the first time she noticed the deep lines of fatigue etched into his face. "You do look as though you've missed a few nights' sleep recently," she commented.

"One or two." He smiled slightly, and his eyes lit up with the warmth Megan found so strangely disconcerting. "I was stationed in Luxembourg until three days ago when I was summoned back to CIA headquarters in Washington. I spent thirty-six hours being debriefed on my Luxembourg assignment and twelve hours being briefed on the situation here. Then I flew to London last night in an army cargo plane. For some reason, the plane was carrying a hundred and five crates of ducklings and me. Have you ever spent seven hours listening to thirteen hundred frightened ducks? I'm beginning to feel as though my supply of energy bailed out somewhere in the middle of the Atlantic."

Megan couldn't help returning his smile. "Why on earth was the U.S. army air-freighting ducks to London?"

"God knows. I didn't dare ask."

She laughed. "You may as well know I'm disappointed in you, Steve. You've shattered one of my favorite illusions. I can't imagine James Bond being defeated by a few crates of livestock."

"James Bond, if you remember, was the creation of somebody's overactive imagination. He only had to keep going for two hundred pages. I have a whole lifetime ahead of me."

"Even so, I thought all CIA agents were supposed to be superjocks. Didn't you go through basic training without any sleep, learning to fight off attackers with lethal karate chops?"

"I guess I flunked that part of basic training. The agency probably only hired me because I got a perfect score on the other part of the test—seducing beautiful enemy agents."

His gaze, faintly quizzical, seemed to linger on Megan's mouth, and she felt her teasing smile fade. The brief moment of harmony vanished, and suddenly she couldn't think of anything appropriate to say. She walked over to the window, wanting an excuse to hide her face from his inspection. "If you're tired, perhaps you'd like to take a nap," she said, and even to her own ears her voice sounded stiff.

"What I'd like is about twelve hours uninterrupted sleep in a comfortable bed. But I'll settle for a quick, cold shower if you're prepared to offer me one."

"Of course. I'll get you some soap and a clean towel."

They walked upstairs, and she removed a large yellow bath towel from the linen closet. Steve's hand reached out to restrain her when she started to walk back downstairs.

"Megan," he said quietly, "I'm trusting you to behave sensibly. The back and front doors are both guarded. If you try to run away, the police constables will stop you. Please understand, you're not under arrest. These precautions have been worked out for your own safety."

"Sure they have!" She jerked her hand away, strongly aware of the imprint of his fingers on her skin and hating herself for the awareness. "You and the inspector are all heart!"

"We don't want you to get hurt," he said quietly.

"That's great news! And I guess the United States government sent you over here by air freight especially to take care of me. The fact that everybody expects me to run off to Moscow with a secret formula tucked into my bra has nothing to do with your sudden desire to *protect* me."

"Protecting the interests of the United States is my job, Megan."

"You sound so sickeningly noble when you say that! Well, don't let *me* keep you from doing your duty. Have a good brisk shower, Agent Callahan, because I wouldn't want you to fall asleep on the job. God knows what vital secrets I might pass on while you're dozing! After all, it's obvious that the Russians are simply dying to get their hands on me. It's easy to understand why they need a librarian whose special field of expertise is Latin documents of the fifteenth century. They probably need me for their space program. Do you think the man in the moon speaks Latin?"

Steve's expression remained maddeningly calm. "Is that your special field?" he asked. "Latin, no less. How impressive!" He went into the bathroom and locked the door behind him with a decisive click.

Megan was pretending to read when he came downstairs, his hair still wet from the shower and the lines of fatigue on his face somewhat diminished. "I feel like a new man," he said. "Almost totally human."

"That's good," she said, fixing her eyes on her book, although the urge to turn and look at him again was almost overwhelming. She couldn't remember feeling such a strong physical attraction to a man since she was fourteen and had fallen madly in love with the high school quarterback. But as far as she was concerned, sexual attraction was an emotion suited only to teenagers. Around the time of her mother's third divorce she had decided never to step onto the sickening roller coaster of passionate love. That was one of the reasons she had been attracted to Jeffrey. She had thought he offered friendship and lasting companionship without the added burden of passion. She was convinced that the brief, blazing attraction of sexual desire was not for her.

Steve broke the lengthening silence. "If your book isn't too fascinating, how about watching the news on TV? I think it would help, Megan, if you knew exactly what was being reported about you and Dr. Brookfield. Sometimes it's better to face up to the worst of a situation right at the beginning."

"What do you mean? What can the television news

possibly say that's so bad?"

"I don't know for sure, of course, but a highly qualified scientist has defected, taking research data about a major new technology with him. He's left behind a young, beautiful American wife who may or may not be about to join him in the Soviet Union. No good reporter can ignore that kind of a story. They want to know if you're going to defect like Jeffrey."

Megan closed her book with an angry snap. "And that's what you really want to know, isn't it?" she said. "You're just like the reporters. You're here to find out if I'm about to defect to the Soviet Union, not to protect me or for any of the other pseudo reasons you've given."

"If you're planning to defect to the Soviet bloc and I manage to stop you, I consider that I've given you the most valuable protection possible," Steve said grimly. "You've never visited Communist Europe. I have. Anybody thinking of emigrating to the Soviet Union should take a quick walk along the Berlin Wall. You can't see much over the coils of barbed wire, but it's a very instructive way to spend the afternoon."

He swung around abruptly and walked over to the television set. He flicked it on, then sat at one end of the sofa without saying anything further. After a moment's hesitation, Megan sat down at the opposite end of the sofa.

The flickering colors of the TV screen consolidated into the rugged features of the evening newscaster. To Megan's relief, Jeffrey's defection was no longer the lead story, and she began to think that Steve had exaggerated the media's interest in her plans.

Her relief was short-lived. The second story was devoted to an update of the events surrounding Jeffrey's defection. The reporters, unable to elicit many hard facts, had evidently decided to concentrate on the human interest angle. And, as far as Megan could judge, they had decided she was the human interest.

In detached silence she watched the film of her brief exchange with Robert Heath. It was hard to identify herself with the Megan Brookfield portrayed on the TV screen. She wondered how the camera could record a scene so accurately and yet tell such a lie. The woman on the television film appeared sensuous, vibrant, and darkly mysterious—everything Megan knew she was not.

The camera suddenly switched angles to record Steve Callahan's hurried arrival in the squad car. Megan's sense of detachment began to waver as she watched herself fall into his arms with a small cry of helplessness. Had she really turned to him with that dewy-eyed look of appeal?

Her detachment vanished entirely as the newscast continued. No wonder the reporters had deserted her front door. They had been too busy interviewing her neighbors, her colleagues—even the owner of the bakery where she bought her bread—to maintain a vigil outside the cottage. Apparently it was considered deeply sinister that she bought a loaf of pumpernickel every Wednesday afternoon at four o'clock. Why didn't she ever eat white bread like most other people? Why did she buy bread only on Wednesdays?

Perhaps her sense of the ridiculous would have come to the rescue if the newscaster hadn't suddenly announced, "And now, courtesy of American television, a satellite interview with Mrs. Delgado of Houston, Texas. Mrs. Delgado is the mother of Megan Brookfield."

Megan felt her body grow rigid with foreboding. Her hands curled tightly around the sofa cushion, but she couldn't make them relax. She knew every trace of color drained out of her cheeks when her mother's image appeared on the screen. Mrs. Delgado, still beautiful at forty-seven, smiled sadly into the camera. In her high, soft voice, with its hint of southern charm, she recounted the mournful litany of Megan, her eldest daughter.

According to her mother, Megan had been a problem child from the moment of her birth. Quiet, not wanting to play with other children, she had spent her school career poring over books and ignoring her brothers and sisters. Her mother had lavished love and affection on her, but to no avail. Some children just wouldn't respond to love. Megan had refused to stay with her mother. She had moved to Washington, D.C., and immediately became involved with all the wrong young men.

At this point in the interview, Mrs. Delgado opened her soft brown eyes very wide and gazed up at her interviewer. Hardened veteran though he was, he was visibly moved by the tears trembling on her long lashes. "When Megan was in college, all her friends were foreigners," Mrs. Delgado said. "And, of course, she left America just as soon as she could. She never did appreciate our wonderful way of life here."

"I understand your daughter went to England as part of her doctoral program," the interviewer said. "That seems a valid reason to leave the States."

For a moment Mrs. Delgado's brown eyes were no longer soft and misty. "But look at what happened after she got to England. She married a Communist spy!" Mrs. Delgado hastily lowered her voice, and her lips quivered pathetically. "I begged her to wait, to come home and find a nice American boy to marry. But Megan was always so headstrong, I knew there was no hope of her listening to me."

"Has your daughter contacted you in the last twenty-four hours, Mrs. Delgado?"

"No." Megan's mother sighed, and two tears spilled over to trickle down her smooth cheeks. She turned directly to the camera, her hands clasped together in a gesture of appeal that would have looked absurd on anybody else. "Megan," she said, "wherever you are, if you see this program, please call me. We all love you, no matter what you've done. Your dear stepfather and I— we want you to come home."

The image of her mother's beautiful, pleading face gradually faded. Megan continued to stare at the television set, but she registered nothing more about the newscast. She was only half aware of Steve getting up and walking quietly across the room to switch off the TV. Even after the final glimmer of light had disappeared, she continued to sit ramrod straight on the sofa, her eyes fixed on the blank gray screen.

She didn't react in any way when Steve sat beside her on the sofa. Subconsciously she must have felt the warmth of his body close to hers, because when he reached out to grasp her hands, she inexplicably started to shiver. His hands tightened slightly around her icy cold fingers. Then, when the shivers refused to stop, he murmured a few reassuring words and took her into his arms.

"Shush," he said softly, one hand smoothing her hair away from her white face, his other arm holding her loosely within its protective circle. "It's all over now, Megan. It's going to be okay."

She scarcely heard what he was saying, and anyway

she could make no sense of his words, but his voice was gentle, and right at that moment she desperately needed to have somebody near her who seemed to care.

"Why does she hate me?" she asked, her voice no more than a harsh whisper. Somehow she didn't doubt that Steve would know she was talking about her mother, although there was no logical reason to assume he had seen through her mother's saccharine sweetness. "What did I ever do to make her hate me so?"

"She probably blames you for being the cause of a marriage she didn't want. You mentioned that she was already pregnant when she married your father. Quite apart from that, you're intelligent, and you're starting to be successful in your career. And if that isn't enough to make her envious, you're more beautiful than she is. I guess, as far as your mother's concerned, that's your worst crime."

His explanation was so ridiculous that Megan's shivering finally stopped. She even managed to produce a tiny smile. "Thank you for the kind lies, Steve," she said with real sincerity. "But I accepted years ago that I'm not particularly attractive. Whatever my mother has against me, I know it isn't that. Didn't you see the way she looks? The way that newscaster was eating out of her hand? And she's nearly forty-eight years old! Why would she be jealous of me?"

Steve's arms were still around her, but as she spoke he held her slightly away from his body, cupping her face in his hands. His palms felt firm and faintly callused against her soft skin. She found herself almost hypnotized by the brilliant cobalt blue of his eyes as he stared down at her, searching her features with a strange intensity.

"You really mean that, don't you?" he asked, his voice

and expression shocked. "Has your mother managed to psych you out to the point that you can't recognize your own attractions? Do you really not know that you're a beautiful woman?"

"Beautiful!" Megan's attempt at a casual laugh didn't quite come off. "I'm too tall," she said. "Haven't you noticed I'm over five feet seven inches? My mother is five two, and my next tallest sister after me is five four. Mom used to call me the family giant. And I'm too thin. Even Jeffrey complained that my..." She closed her eyes for a moment, but when she opened them again she had managed to fix a bright smile firmly in place. "Well, anyway, everybody agrees I'm too thin," she repeated.

Steve brushed his thumb very gently across her mouth. "Haven't you heard the saying that you can't ever be too rich or too thin? Besides, you don't seem all that slender to me. No jutting hipbones or hollow cheeks." His gaze was deliberately provocative as it roamed over her breasts. "In fact, in my highly expert judgment, you seem to curve in all the right places."

For some reason his teasing remarks didn't embarrass her. Some of the pain caused by her mother's appearance on the newscast began to drain away. She looked directly into Steve's eyes and saw genuine friendliness lingering there behind the laughter. Maybe in his effort to be kind he wasn't being truthful about her physical attractions, but he was doing a great job of restoring her shattered morale.

"Thanks, Steve," she said huskily.

"You're welcome." His eyes still reflected nothing but warmth and teasing reassurance. He continued to hold her face cupped between his hands, but she felt no tension in the contact. It seemed entirely natural, no more than a friendly gesture, when he bent his head to drop a quick, light kiss on her lips.

His mouth brushed against hers, soft, casual, and undemanding. At the brief contact a streak of cold flame seemed to twist through Megan's body. After a second or so, he lifted his head, and she saw all of her own astonishment reflected in Steve's darkened gaze. Neither of them moved as they stared at one another in complete silence.

Still without saying anything, Steve reached out and twisted one hand through the long, dark strands of her hair, while his other hand slipped around her waist, drawing her tight against his chest. She realized with a silent gasp of amazement that he was going to kiss her again.

He bent his head slowly, as if he couldn't quite believe what he was doing. Then his mouth covered hers, pressing against her lips in a kiss that was hot, urgent, and fiercely demanding.

At first, she was too stunned to resist. His arms tightened around her, and his hands spread out along the length of her spine, molding her against his body. He caressed her mouth seductively, so that she parted her lips without quite knowing how or why it had happened. When she felt his tongue thrusting against hers, her body reacted with a sharp ache of unfamiliar excitement.

For a few bewildering seconds she was lost in a dream world of physical pleasure. Harsh reality seemed a thousand miles away, and only the magic touch of Steve's mouth on hers had any meaning. She thought how wonderful it would be to stay locked in his arms forever.

The intimacy of his kiss deepened, and awareness of what she was actually doing returned in a blinding, painful flash. She pulled herself out of his grasp, stumbling up from the sofa and hurrying toward the door.

"It's time to make dinner," she said. In the context of what had just happened between them the remark was ridiculous, but Megan's brain felt as if it had gone on vacation.

"That seems like a good idea," Steve said. He walked over to the window and stared out into the twilight. His voice sounded mocking, but she couldn't see his expression. "The reporters have all gone," he said abruptly. "Go ahead and make something to eat. I'll join you after I've had a word with the police constables. They'll be going off duty soon." He strode toward the front door without waiting to hear her reply.

Megan walked slowly into the kitchen and stood staring blankly at the kitchen sink. After a while the throb of her pulses subsided, and she was able to think about practical, everyday matters again. She searched inside the refrigerator until she found the pork chops she had bought to cook for Jeffrey's dinner. With her usual impeccable tidiness, she spread waxed paper on the kitchen counter and dipped the chops neatly into seasoned bread crumbs before putting them into a heated, buttered pan. It was strange to think that Jeffrey would probably be eating his dinner in Moscow, a thousand miles away, while Steve Callahan, an agent of the United States federal government, was about to sit at Jeffrey's table and eat Jeffrey's pork chops.

Megan opened the small freezer compartment of the refridgerator and looked for a package of frozen vegetables. This wasn't the time, she decided, to start worrying about the subtle ironies that life could produce. She was allowing the traumas of the past couple of days to get to her. She liked gentle, introspective men who didn't try to make raw, sexual appeal the basis of a relationship. She had never respected men like Steve Callahan, who seemed to view the whole world in terms of physical action. That sort of man reminded her too strongly of her mother's lovers.

She added the frozen broccoli spears to a pot of boiling water, taking care not to splash the stove. She had always survived difficult personal situations by concentrating on the hard, cold facts. And the crucial fact about the current situation was that she was a suspect and Steve was her jailer. Now, she reminded herself, was definitely not an appropriate moment to change the habits of a lifetime.

Chapter Five

THE HOT BISCUITS—SCONES, as Megan had learned to call them since her arrival in England—were flaky and delicious. The pork chops were cooked to perfection, and the spears of broccoli tasted as good as frozen vegetables possibly could. Nevertheless, dinner was an uncomfortable meal.

Steve complimented Megan on her superb cooking, then carefully directed the conversation into neutral channels. But she found it hard to concentrate on their desultory discussion of popular art exhibitions and their favorite baseball teams. As soon as the meal was over, she escaped back to the kitchen, refusing Steve's offer to help clear away the dishes.

It was only a little after eight o'clock when she returned to the living room and told him she was going to bed. "I guess you can leave now," she said, taking care to avoid looking at him. "Where are you going to stay? Did somebody book you a local hotel, or are you going back to London?"

He turned around, forcing her by sheer exertion of willpower to meet his gaze head on. "You know better than that, Megan," he said quietly. "You know I have to spend the night here."

"No, I don't know any such thing! You and your agency have no reasonable grounds for insisting that I have to be watched twenty-four hours a day! I've told you before I'm not about to run off to Moscow the minute your back's turned."

"It's true we have no grounds for suspecting you personally," he said, still in the same deliberately restrained voice. "But we do have considerable evidence from past cases on which to base our judgment. Once the husband defects, it's usually only a matter of time before the wife follows. Until we've had a chance to review the specific evidence about you and Dr. Brookfield, it's essential to ensure that you don't make the security forces of England and the United States look foolish. You're a potentially valuable piece of propaganda, Megan."

"I'm not a piece of anything, I'm a *person!*" She clenched her teeth, hating to repeat the humiliating facts of her relationship with Jeffrey. "I've told you before, I'm not even Jeffrey's wife. Why on earth would I want to follow him when he's deceived me so badly?"

"People in love do strange things." He stood up, and she was aware of the tight lines of strain etched around his mouth. "Besides, we only have your word for it that Dr. Brookfield was already married when he went through that wedding ceremony with you."

She let out her breath in a long, soft sigh. "I see," she said. "You think I'm lying about everything, don't you?" She turned away so that he wouldn't notice how close she was to tears of anger and frustration. "Was that what the little seduction scene before dinner was all about? A carefully calculated test to see how far I was prepared to go in order to throw you off the scent?"

"No."

She was infuriated by his monosyllabic response. "Well, I guess you're right, there's nothing more to be said. Where are you planning to sleep, Mr. Callahan? At the foot of my bed? I don't suppose I have any choice in the matter, so I may as well find out the worst."

"I don't think it's necessary to share your bedroom, Megan. I'll spend the night down here. I have some paperwork to catch up on."

"Paperwork? Don't you mean reports on me, Mr. Callahan? Surely you have to hand in your official assessment of how likely I am to cut and run?"

"Yes," he said laconically. "I'm required to turn in something like that."

His continuing calm infuriated her. "Aren't you afraid I'll creep out the back door while you're writing your report, or tie my sheets together and climb out the window? God knows what a desperate spy like me might get up to once I've escaped from your eagle-eyed surveillance!"

His gaze met hers, direct and deliberately challenging. "Even after a couple of wakeful nights, Megan, I'm a very light sleeper. I don't think you have much chance of leaving the house without disturbing me. You're welcome to try, of course, if you want to put me to the test."

"I've no desire to test *any* of your secret agent skills, Mr. Callahan. The sample before dinner was more than enough for me." She swung around, thrusting her hands into the pockets of her jeans where he wouldn't see that they were shaking. "Just make sure that you don't get restless in the middle of the night and wander in the direction of my bedroom. I'm not interested in finding out how terrific you are at seducing enemy agents, which I believe you boasted was one of your special skills."

There was a short, tense pause. "You know damn well I was joking when I said that," he replied curtly. "You must also know damn well that the CIA doesn't train its operatives to seduce anybody, enemy agents or otherwise."

"I don't know anything about the CIA or MI 6—or any other intelligence organization, for that matter, but I don't expect you to believe me." She swung away, angrier than she was rationally entitled to be. "Good night, Mr. Callahan, I'll see you in the morning."

"I'm going back to London in the morning," he said, his words clipped. "Another agent will be here to replace me."

Megan stopped in her tracks. Her heart lurched unexpectedly, but she refused to acknowledge the jolt. Why should she care if Steve went out of her life as quickly as he had entered it? She lifted her shoulders in a casual shrug. "Then I suppose this is good-bye, not good night." She was pleased that her voice sounded steady, almost indifferent.

He didn't say anything, just inclined his head in the briefest of nods.

There was a momentary pause. "I'll bring you a blanket," she said, jerking her head away from his remote

Refuge In His Arms 71

gaze. "It gets cold here at night, even though it's almost June." She hurried out of the room, eager to escape from a silence that seemed to be pounding painfully against her ears.

She returned within a couple of minutes, holding out a pillow and two lightweight plaid blankets. "Here you are," she said.

He accepted the covers, taking care to avoid touching her hands. "Thank you." His gaze lingered for a moment on her mouth, and she felt her lips part in a totally involuntary reaction.

Abruptly he turned and began spreading the blankets over the sofa. "Good-bye, Megan," he said softly. "Sleep well."

Sleep, however, proved elusive, and it was the early hours of the morning before she finally dropped off. When she came downstairs for breakfast the next morning she discovered that Steve, true to his word, had already left the cottage. She told herself she was glad he had gone.

His duties had been taken over by a middle-aged woman police officer from Scotland Yard's Special Branch. She introduced herself as Sergeant Mary Jenkins and Megan had to suppress a faint feeling of desolation as she glanced at the woman's official identification card. There wasn't a single good reason why she should wish Steve Callahan was still around, and no reason at all for her to trust him. She had watched her mother in the throes of innumerable disastrous love affairs, and she knew that involvement with a man meant nothing except sorrow and heartache—and angry, degrading scenes. Her father's final marriage was successful, she knew, because his third wife was little more than a domestic slave who had traded every ounce of her independence in exchange for the financial security Megan's father provided.

Her own experience with Jeffrey had reinforced her conviction that all men were exploitative and deceptive in their relationships with women. Nothing that Steve had said or done was reason to alter opinions she had held since adolescence, particularly since she seemed to be such a bad judge of character where men were concerned. She had been certain when she married Jeffrey that he respected her as a friend. Now, less than two months later, she knew the truth. Jeffrey had never cared for her. Like her mother and her various stepfathers, he had found nothing about her worthy of love. He had married her only to use her as a convenient pawn in some complex game of international intrigue.

Megan resolutely overcame the beginnings of self-pity as she prepared coffee and a fresh grapefruit for her breakfast. She had made several close friends in high school and in college, and they had all remained in touch even though their careers and marriages had taken them to cities thousands of miles apart. Maybe she didn't have a husband, but she was lucky enough to be able to claim nine or ten really good friends. How many people could say as much? From now on, she decided, she was going to stop worrying about her relationships with the opposite sex and concentrate on her friends and her career.

Megan began to eat her grapefruit. The policewoman sat down at the kitchen table opposite her, accepting Megan's offer of a cup of coffee with a single polite word of thanks. Sergeant Jenkins, Megan had already discovered, was impeccably polite, but not at all communicative. It was going to be difficult to survive several hours of such unnerving, blank-faced companionship.

The phone rang, and the sergeant answered the call. She listened for a few moments, then said, "Hold on, please," and handed the phone to Megan. "It's from your boss," she said. It was the longest sentence she had spoken since introducing herself.

Megan's boss, the chief librarian at the college, was clearly in a state of high agitation. He cleared his throat several times before starting to speak coherently. In view of all the publicity, he said, and in view of the crowds of reporters who had disrupted the routine of the library the day before, he thought it would be better if Mrs. Brookfield didn't come into work "for a while." She would be paid, he hastened to add, but he thought a few weeks' leave of absence would be "in the best interests of all the people concerned."

Megan tried to protest, but in the end she accepted that she wasn't going to be allowed back inside the college library without a long, acrimonious battle. At the moment not even her job seemed worth fighting for. For two days she had been living with her nerves constantly at fever pitch, and now she felt drained of energy. She simply didn't have the stamina to fight against the edicts of the university bureaucracy.

She hung up the phone, pushing the remainder of her grapefruit away with a faint feeling of nausea. It had been quite obvious to her from the tone of the chief librarian's conversation that he had watched last night's television news with avid attention. He clearly expected her to take off for Moscow on the next available flight. No doubt pocketing a few of his precious fifteenth-century manuscripts on the way, she thought wryly, torn between anger and dismay at the Alice in Wonderland absurdity of her situation. He and Steve seemed to have a similar inflated opinion of the Russians' desire for medieval Latin manuscripts. She pushed the thought of Steve Callahan away, trying to concentrate on the practical problem of what she was to do with herself for an entire day of captivity.

She invented a great many small chores, but the day proved a long one. Only one police constable was on duty outside the cottage, and reporters constantly appeared at the back door. Despite Sergeant Jenkins's taciturn manner, Megan was quite glad to have her around to ward off the persistent questions of the journalists. The long, dreary afternoon was finally brightened by a phone call from her American friend, Sally Johansen.

She had been expecting the call. Sally had attended the same high school and the same college as Megan, although their studies had followed different tracks. Sally was a nurse, trained to work with infants born prematurely. At twenty-seven, she was already considered an expert on neonatal nursing care.

She was visiting London for a medical conference, and they had a long-standing arrangement to meet in town this weekend. The conference did not start until Monday morning, and Sally had flown in two days early especially to spend time with Megan. The packed suitcase that Steve Callahan had discovered when he searched the cottage— and had considered so suspicious—had been prepared with Sally's visit in mind.

Sally seemed surprised when her phone call was intercepted by Sergeant Jenkins, but it was clear from her opening remarks that she hadn't heard the news about Jeffrey.

"Do you know how many telephone operators I had

to go through to get to you?" she asked cheerfully when she was finally allowed to speak to Megan. "Hasn't anybody in this country heard of automation or direct dialing?"

"I think they have," Megan replied cautiously, wondering how on earth she was supposed to set about telling her best friend that her husband of two months had turned out to be a spy. She searched frantically for the appropriate words, but none came.

"Er... how are you, Sally?" she said in the end. "Did you have a good flight?"

"Terrific! I love planes. You always get to talk to such fascinating people. The woman sitting next to me was eighty-six years old and taking her first flight. She was coming to England to see her new great-great-grandson who was born last month. One of her great-granddaughters married an Englishman who owns a village pub in Berkshire."

Sally was clearly in possession of her fellow passenger's entire life history, which didn't surprise Megan a bit. Her friend invariably attracted confidences the way a field of summer clover attracted bees. Almost without pausing for breath, Sally continued.

"So how soon can you get into town, Meg? My flight landed at Heathrow Airport at some ungodly hour this morning. and I've already slept for five hours. I'm raring to go."

"Haven't you ever heard of jet lag? You're supposed to take it easy the first night in a new place."

"Nurses are accustomed to working around the clock. Besides, I took one look at London, and my adrenaline started to flow in megadoses. This sure is a fantastic city. No wonder you want to live here! I've decided I have a passion for guys with a British accent. They sound so marvelously uptight; I keep imagining how they must be in bed when they finally decide to let go of all those inhibitions! I can't wait to meet your husband," she added, the connection in her thoughts being all too obvious to Megan. "Although you know you always relied on me to check out your dates. You should never have married Jeff until I had a chance to give him the official once-over!"

"No, I probably shouldn't have." Megan choked off a gasp of nervous laughter, trying to keep her voice suitably light and friendly when she spoke again. She didn't want Sally to think she was begging for sympathy. "I'll do my best to get up to town tomorrow, Sally, but I don't think I'm going to make it tonight. Something's kind of... come up."

Obviously her attempt at casualness didn't come off, because Sally's voice was immediately concerned.

"Meg, what is it? What's happened? Is something wrong with you? With Jeffrey?"

"You might say that. Oh, Lord, Sally, this would be so much easier if you'd already heard the news, but you never could find time to read a newspaper, could you?"

"I've told you before why I don't bother. They never say anything interesting. Once a year I pick one up, and it always says the same thing it said last time I looked: the government has messed up its economic planning, the latest round of international disarmament talks is on the brink of failing, and somebody's just published a new diet book that's a runaway best-seller. Who needs to spend thirty cents a day to find that out?"

As Sally spoke, Megan felt her throat tighten with a sense of loss. Her friend was easygoing and warm-hearted, but how would she react to the news that Megan's husband had turned out to be a traitor? Would she believe that Megan had had no idea what was going on? Part of Megan longed for the comfort of Sally's presence. Another part of her dreaded revealing what a mess she had managed to make of her life, dreaded the possibility of her best friend's rejection. Megan drew in a deep breath, steeling herself to face up to what might come.

"I guess I'm going to have to tell you straight out what's happened. I wish I could think of some way to make this sound less incredible, Sally, but I can't. My husband...Jeffrey...has defected to the Soviet Union. The police think he's taken some valuable scientific information with him. In case you're wondering, I'm not planning to go after him."

For once, even Sally was stunned into total silence.

"My God!" she said at last. "That scientist they were talking about is *your* husband! Oh, my God, why didn't I pay attention to last night's news? Meg, do you want me to come and stay with you? Is there anything I can do to help?"

Only when she relaxed her convulsive grip on the phone did Megan realize just how afraid of Sally's rejection she had been. "Thanks for the offer," she said softly, "but I'd prefer to come up to town, if I can. I need to get away, Sal."

"Of course, I can understand that. But why should there be any trouble in getting away? Just toss a toothbrush and some clean underwear into a bag and come."

"The police are here. I'm not...I'm not allowed to leave the cottage."

There was only the tiniest pause before Sally spoke again. "Tell me exactly what's been happening," she said, her voice authoritative. "I know you, Megan, and I'll bet you've been keeping all your problems to yourself while you're breaking apart inside. Lord, no wonder you were so attracted to England. You must have British genes somewhere in your ancestry. Anybody knowing you would think you'd invented the stiff upper lip."

Megan gave a brief, much edited account of Jeffrey's hurried departure and the events that had followed. She decided that it would be irrelevant to mention Steve Callahan's name and the fact that he had been sent over by the CIA. Sally was full of sympathy, giving no indication that she thought Megan was a fool for swallowing Jeffrey's lies. For the first time in three days, Megan began to feel that perhaps she wasn't a criminal or an idiot to have contracted a bigamous marriage with a traitor— merely an unfortunate victim. The relief from self-accusation renewed her flagging mental energy. She promised to fight for permission to visit London on Saturday, saying she would call Sally back as soon as she won official approval.

She had almost given up hope when Inspector Browning telephoned to say she could meet her friend for lunch in London, but she couldn't stay overnight. A police car would be provided, together with a plainclothes police escort who would accompany her to lunch. Before hanging up, the inspector informed Megan politely that she would be sent a bill for the cost of the car and for the agent's lunch, since they were extra expenses incurred strictly for her convenience.

Megan actually laughed, her sense of humor returning at the prospect of spending a whole day away from the confinement of the cottage. "It will be cheap at the price," she said. "I never knew how much I disliked this cottage until now."

"I thought it seemed a nice place myself," the inspector said. His good-bye sounded friendly. "Enjoy your day out, Mrs. Brookfield...er, Ms. Richards."

She dressed with special care the next morning, determined to put the insecurities of her marriage behind her. She wanted to look good for this meeting with Sally, and, now that Jeffrey was no longer at her side, undermining her fragile self-confidence, she was prepared to believe that she could make herself look as attractive as the next woman.

She swept her hair back in a lustrous, sophisticated chignon and wore a tailored, peacock green suit with a pencil-slim skirt and a short matching jacket. She slipped her feet into black shoes with high, slender heels and tucked a matching black leather purse under her arm.

Aside from wanting to look good when she saw Sally for the first time in more than two years, Megan had another reason for her careful grooming. She was well aware that, in visiting a London hotel, she was running the risk of being spotted by a keen-eyed reporter. If any more pictures of her appeared in the press, she was determined to ensure that they portrayed the image she wanted to convey: a woman who was cool, dignified, and in command of herself.

It was the middle of the morning when the redoubtable Sergeant Jenkins knocked on her bedroom door and announced that the police car had arrived, ready to drive her to London. The sergeant escorted her downstairs and out the kitchen door without saying a word. Megan swallowed a gasp when she saw the plainsclothes police escort

Inspector Browning had insisted upon providing. He was leaning against the door of a gray, unmarked squad car with an apparent indolence that barely masked the alertness of his lean, muscled body.

He straightened as soon as the kitchen door closed behind her, walking forward and unlatching the garden gate. "Hello, Megan," Steve Callahan said. "Are you ready for your trip to town?"

Chapter Six

SHE ALMOST STUMBLED as she walked down the narrow flight of stone steps, but she recovered her balance and walked along the short garden path to the back gate without any other outward sign of shock. Courteously he closed the gate behind her and opened the door to the passenger side of the car.

She barely glanced at him, although she noticed that this morning he looked startlingly attractive in a conservative dark gray business suit. She wasn't the only person who'd decided to dress up, she thought distractedly.

None of her whirlwind emotions showed in her voice. "Good morning, Agent Callahan," she said coolly. She turned her back on him as she held out her hand to the policewoman, who remained inside the small back garden. "Good-bye, Sergeant Jenkins. Will you still be here when I get back?"

"Probably not, Mrs. Brookfield. Good-bye for now." The sergeant shook her hand in a brief, firm clasp, and the total impassivity of her features was brightened for a second or two by a polite smile.

Steve murmured his own good-bye, then slid into the driver's seat and turned on the ignition. The devastating, teasing gleam of humor reappeared in his eyes. "I must remember to tell Inspector Browning that I saw the sergeant smile with my own eyes and heard her speak at least six consecutive words, three of them unnecessary. I believe that's an official record."

Megan totally ignored his remarks. She stared out of the side window as he reversed the car along the narrow lane behind the cottage. "Why are you here?" she asked curtly.

"To drive you to London. I understand you're meeting an old school friend."

"You know what I mean. Why have *you* come? Why not another policeman from Special Branch?"

"I volunteered for the job," he said shortly. "Scotland Yard is as short-staffed as every other police department."

There seemed nothing more to say. She kept her face averted, watching the familiar countryside flash by the car window. She couldn't stop her emotions from churning with irrational fervor, but she had learned long ago to control her thoughts. Concentrate on the here and now, she reminded herself, staring out at the green early summer landcape.

In the short time she had been in England, she had

come to love the sight of oddly shaped fields surrounded by tall hedges, gentle hills, and small copses of trees disappearing into the gray horizon. The spectacular beauty of the United States often gave the impression of being untamed. Here in England, on the other hand, the fields were so carefully landscaped that they seemed to be part of a Constable painting, designed to look rustic and appealing rather than to be functional. She knew, however, that appearances were deceptive. English farmers were among the most efficient in Europe, however toylike their fields might appear. And—at the other end of the scale—American farmers usually had Mother Nature thoroughly under control despite the rugged vastness of the land they worked on.

Nothing is ever precisely what it seems, she reflected, unable to hold back a sigh. She grimaced with a touch of impatient self-mockery. Oh, boy, you're really into philosophy these days, she thought.

Steve obviously heard her sigh, for he glanced away from the road. "Would you like to hear what I was doing yesterday?" he asked. "Inspector Browning and I were coordinating research into Dr. Brookfield's past. We discovered some interesting facts about him."

Her head jerked up. "What?" she asked. "What have you found out?"

"Well, for a start, the documents he used to get into Cambridge as an undergraduate were forgeries. In fact, we've found no legitimate records for Jeffrey Brookfield prior to his admission to the university."

"But I saw his birth certificate! I saw it when we applied to get married."

"His birth certificate is definitely a forgery. His parents were listed on the certificate as Jean and Arthur

Brookfield. They existed, and they were killed in a motorway accident, as he claimed, but they had no children. He didn't attend the high school he said he attended, either."

"Then Jeffrey wasn't really Dr. Jeffrey Brookfield at all?"

"The doctoral degree is genuine, although the name isn't. Everything he's done in the last twenty years since he was eighteen is on record, and that record would be difficult to forge. He's been working within a very narrow, scientific community where everybody knows everybody else in the same field of research." Steve fell silent for a moment as he edged the car through some heavy traffic.

"I know Jeffrey told you he was thirty-eight, Megan," he said when they had a clear road ahead of them again. "But if you hadn't known how old he was, what age would you have guessed him to be?"

She was surprised by his question, but she tried to answer it objectively. "It's hard to pinpoint anybody's age within a couple of years," she said at last. "But I suppose Jeffrey struck me as looking older than thirty-eight. His hair was thinning, and he had lots of lines around his eyes. But men often start to lose their hair when they're in their twenties, and some people wrinkle more easily than others. Plus Jeffrey spent a lot of time working with intricate scientific equipment, which must be a strain on the eyes. It's not surprising that his back was a little stooped and his forehead had a few lines on it."

"Perhaps not."

"What was the significance of your question?"

He looked at her searchingly for a moment or two.

"It's a theory I'm working on," he said finally.

She was hurt by his reluctance to admit her into his confidence, and she shrugged, turning away to stare out of the car window again. Steve eventually broke the lengthening silence.

"We ran a routine check on Dr. Brookfield's closest associates. We came up with some fascinating stuff on Helen Meaney, the assistant you mentioned to us."

There was no point in trying to pretend she wasn't interested. "What did you find out about her?" she asked. "Dr. Meaney struck me as the sort of woman who'd have no life at all outside her work at the lab."

"'No life at all' just about sums it up. What's more, her papers are forged, like Jeffrey's. There's no record of her past before she turns up as an applicant to Bristol University—the year after Jeffrey appeared at Cambridge. Inspector Browning is driving to Cambridge to interview her at the lab this morning. As you can imagine, we're hoping she'll help us clear up a lot of loose ends."

"You can't hope it more than I do," Megan said fervently. "I hope she has an answer for every one of your loose ends."

They made good time and completed the drive to town in just over an hour. Sally was staying at one of the prestigious old London hotels situated on Park Lane. Steve left the car in an underground garage; apparently he was quite familiar with London traffic and parking problems.

"I've spent several months in England at one time or another," he said in response to Megan's comment. "Where did you arrange to meet your friend?"

"In the main dining room," she said.

They walked across the busy street and into the lobby

of the hotel, the touch of his hand underneath her elbow strictly impersonal. They waited for the elevator with a crowd of Arab businessmen, who wore the flowing white robes of the East but carried English leather briefcases. Steve spoke quietly, so that only Megan could hear him.

"I know Sally's your oldest friend. But please be discreet in what you say to her."

"I think I've already told you, Mr. Callahan, that I have no intention of telling the truth about my so-called marriage to anybody. I have no desire to convince my friends I'm a fool."

They rode the elevator in silence. Sally, for once, was punctual. She smiled radiantly when she saw Megan, hugging her close for several minutes before subjecting Steve to a quick, approving appraisal.

"Hi! I'm Sally Johansen, an old friend of Megan's," she said, shaking his hand. Her short brown hair curled as riotously as ever around her thin, piquant face, and her tiny body was still perfectly proportioned. Megan had always admired her friend's petite prettiness.

"I'm Steve Callahan. It's good to meet you, Sally."

"You're a friend of Megan's? Not from college, or I would know you."

Megan saw Steve's look of enquiry, and she was grateful to him for his unexpected display of tact. He was leaving it up to her to decide whether or not to reveal that he was an agent from the CIA, working on a federal government case.

"Steve's a recent friend." She heard herself speak the words almost before she was aware of making any decision about what she would say. "He's been doing a great job of protecting me from the press. I'm grateful to him."

"Some reporters can't seem to tell the difference between harassment and justifiable curiosity," Steve said easily. "Why don't we find ourselves a comfortable corner table, and then you two can gossip to your heart's content. You can ignore me. I've heard the food here is excellent, and I'm planning to check it out."

The dining room was more crowded than Megan expected it to be. For a second or two, while she waited for the maître d' to conduct them to a table, she had the unpleasant impression that all conversation stopped and every eye turned toward her. The impression was only momentary. The maître d' led them to a table by the window, and the buzz of lunchtime chatter quickly resumed. You'd better watch out, Megan warned herself. Less than two months of living with Jeffrey, and you're becoming paranoid.

Steve seemed to be aware of her constraint, although in the past her dates had often commented on how hard it was to read what she was thinking. She was relieved when he took charge of the conversation, asking Sally about her career and the convention she was planning to attend. He was obviously interested in her specialty, probing gently into her feelings about working in an area of medicine where so many of the infant patients inevitably died.

"Yes, but when we save a baby, it's such a fantastic high for all of us it almost compensates for the bad times," Sally said. "If you'd ever seen a mother's face when she holds her premature baby outside the incubator for the first time, you'd understand what I'm talking about. And nurses know how important their care is to the baby. Surgery and advanced medical techniques can only do so much. Unless a premature baby is with nurses who really care, he or she seems to lose the will to live. Human beings can't survive without love, whatever age they are; I'm quite sure of that. I've proven it over and over again in my profession."

The waiter came to take their order, and his intrusion seemed to remind Sally that the conversation so far had been exclusively between her and Steve. She turned quickly to Megan and began to ask sympathetic questions about her friend's brief marriage to Jeffrey.

Even if Steve hadn't warned her to be discreet, Megan couldn't have told her friend the whole truth, so she wove a tale of half-truths and innuendo that she hoped would somehow serve to explain the inexplicable. She was intensely conscious of Steve's silent presence at the table, and sometimes she felt that she was justifying her actions to him rather than describing them to Sally. She knew she would never be able to tell anyone of the systematic, sadistic pleasure Jeffrey had taken in abusing her. His abuse had never been physical, only verbal: constant, barbed attacks on her personality and appearance that alternated with long periods of total silence. After two months of such treatment, she had begun to wonder if physical mistreatment might not almost be easier to bear.

Any tiny shreds of self-confidence that were left over after his verbal attacks he had systematically demolished in the darkness of their bedroom. Megan had never expected to feel overwhelming physical desire for her husband. She had never wanted to experience the sort of emotional abandonment she had seen her mother indulge in. She had not, however, expected to find herself so appalled by Jeffrey's sexual advances that any response became impossible. She soon discovered her mistake. Within a week of their marriage, Jeffrey had declared she was frigid. Before he left her, Megan had begun to believe he was right.

She was explaining to Sally how little time she had actually spent with Jeffrey when their lunch arrived, providing a welcome excuse to stop talking. After the waiter had left, Sally reached out and squeezed her friend's hand.

"You always were a sucker for the underdog, Meg, and Jeffrey took advantage of that. But you have to put the past behind you. Your marriage is over, through no fault of yours. Be realistic, Meg. Apply for a divorce, and then forget about Jeffrey. Believe me, he's not worth remembering."

Megan drew in a deep breath, deciding suddenly to admit that she had no need to get a divorce since her marriage to Jeffrey had never been legal. She felt uncomfortable about leaving so many lingering half-truths lying between her best friend and herself. She looked up and saw Steve shake his head in a brief, almost imperceptible, gesture. She fell silent, surprised that he had so accurately interpreted her intentions, and he immediately took command of the conversation once again.

"Here comes the waiter with our wine," he said. "I ordered some champagne. I thought your first trip outside the States deserved a toast, Sally." He waited while the waiter expertly popped the cork and served each of them; then he raised his glass in a laughing salute. "I hope your trip is everything you want it to be, Sally, professionally and personally."

"Why, thank you, Steve," she replied. Her cheeks were flushed a becoming shade of rosy pink, and her brown eyes were frankly admiring as she touched her glass to Steve's. She took a generous swallow of champagne and smiled mischievously at him over the rim of her glass. "As a matter of fact, things are looking better by the minute!"

He grinned. "I was thinking the same thing myself."

Megan took a large swallow of champagne, thrusting away a totally irrational spurt of jealousy. Why, in heaven's name, did it matter that Steve and Sally were so obviously hitting it off? Sally was a success with virtually every man she met, and Steve was exactly the type of man who appealed to her. Unbidden, the thought sprang into her mind that Steve was the type of man who appealed to most women. It was hard for women to resist that alluring hint of dark, smoldering sensuality hidden just beneath a tanned, studiedly casual exterior. Hard for most women but not for her, Megan thought, taking a hasty bite of cold salmon and another swig of champagne. As far as she was concerned, Steve was a hostile CIA agent and nothing more.

Sally and Steve were comparing notes about a Broadway musical they had both seen. Megan saw the sparkle animating her friend's attractive features, and the fierce flash of jealousy returned. She immediately damped it down, allowing her gaze to wander around the room while she tried to collect her cool.

Her attempt was unsuccessful. One glance around the dining room was enough to show her that the other restaurant patrons were staring avidly at her table. Moreover, everybody glanced furtively away as soon as she looked in their direction. Nobody wanted to meet her eyes.

Megan felt a hot flush of color rush up into her cheeks. It had been crazy to eat in such a public place, with all the publicity given to Jeffrey's defection. She had probably been recognized the moment she walked into the hotel. The sudden silence when she entered the dining room hadn't been her imagination, after all. Only the good manners of the restaurant patrons had kept their curiosity within reasonable limits. In another, less dignified hotel, the guests would probably have rushed up and asked for her autograph. She wasn't quite as newsworthy as a movie star, of course, but she knew that criminals were often treated as celebrities.

With new awareness she looked methodically around the room and saw the same eager curiosity on almost every face. You could say one thing for television, she thought wearily. It certainly made for instant recognition and notoriety. For some reason her gaze was drawn to a table in the far corner of the restaurant and, with a sinking heart, she recognized one of the journalists who had waited outside her cottage two days earlier. As soon as he caught her eye, he stood up and began to walk toward her.

She reacted instinctively, determined to get away before he could reach their table and completely ruin her lunch with Sally by his endless, probing questions.

"Excuse me," she said, cutting into the middle of Steve's anecdote. "I have to go to the ladies' room. I'll be right back."

Their table was by a window. The rest rooms were on the other side of the dining room, screened by a long row of tall potted palms and thick flowering shrubs in dark brown tubs. She hurried across the room and slipped behind the greenery, hoping that the reporter couldn't see her. She uttered a silent prayer of thanks that rest rooms still constituted a final, unbreachable bastion of sexual segregation. The reporter wouldn't follow her into the ladies' room, however brash and aggressive he might be.

The room was almost deserted. She brushed her hair and ran cold water over her wrists, taking a long time to renew her lip gloss even though she knew she couldn't hide away forever. She had already been gone for over five minutes. Any second now Steve would be sending Sally to find out what had happened to her. He was probably wondering if she'd climbed out a convenient window and taken off for Moscow, Megan thought with a touch of bitter humor. That was how heroines in the movies always seemed to escape from their guards. Somehow, even if the bathroom had contained a window, she didn't think it would be quite that easy to get rid of Steve.

She left the ladies' room reluctantly. The tall potted plants successfully screened her from the sight of the people eating in the restaurant, but they also blocked her view of the dining room. Unless she went up close to the bushes and peered through the foilage, she couldn't see Steve and Sally on the other side of the room, so she had no way of knowing if the reporter had come across to their table. She hesitated for another second or so, and then realized how crazy it was to stand outside the rest room door, lurking behind the potted palms. The reporter couldn't force her to answer his questions and, if he was misguided enough to create an unpleasant scene, the hotel management would almost certainly ask him to leave.

She was suddenly aware that while she had been dithering two men had quietly approached and now stood, one on either side of her, suffocatingly close to her body.

Refuge In His Arms

Oh, damn, she thought. More reporters. "Excuse me," she said stiffly, allowing her anger to show. She started to walk away.

Both men reached out simultaneously and grabbed her arms. "Mrs. Brookfield, we would like to talk to you," one of them said.

"Let go of my arms!" she demanded. "I certainly don't want to talk to you! I don't know what newspaper you're from, but if you don't let me go, I swear I'll sue it and you for every penny you possess."

The men didn't bother to answer. They responded by edging closer to her, making it impossible for her to move. "We are not reporters," one of them said. "Please continue walking toward the door, Mrs. Brookfield. We do not wish to attract attention, and we have a message for you."

Her throat constricted with fear, and she tried again to pull herself away from the men, but they were like iron pillars wedging her between their bodies, clamping her arms to her sides.

"Our message is from Jeffrey, Mrs. Brookfield. He has sent us to fetch you. He urgently wishes to communicate with you."

"I have nothing to say to Jeffrey," she said through clenched teeth. "Not now, not ever, and you can tell him that from me."

"Jeffrey has sent us to find you, Mrs. Brookfield. He wishes to see you."

"Well, I don't want to see him! Just let go of me, will you? If you don't, I'll scream."

She felt the prod of something hard against her waist. "That wouldn't be wise, Mrs. Brookfield. Please don't scream. Just keep walking."

They have guns, she thought, almost paralyzed with fear. They must have guns in their pockets. Her stomach was a hollow void, and her legs trembled so violently that only the support of her two captors kept her upright. She had never before realized physical fear was a sensation you could taste, like sickness in the back of your throat.

When she saw Steve only a few yards away from her, the relief was so great that for a moment she couldn't speak. She was just about to scream out his name when he swung around, as if sensing her presence. He started to run toward her, and suddenly she was free, her captors no longer restraining her. Her wobbly legs wouldn't move. She stood where she was, rooted to the spot until Steve caught her in his arms just in time to prevent her from falling.

"Megan!" he exclaimed in a hoarse whisper. "My God, Megan, are you all right?" As he spoke, his hands were already running over her body in a quick, thorough appraisal. "They didn't hurt you?" He pulled off her jacket and undid the top button of her blouse.

"Get some water, will you?" he asked Sally, who had hurried to join them. "She looks as though she's about to faint."

Megan said nothing. She was concentrating all her energy on stopping her teeth from chattering. The fright was still with her even though the men had gone. Steve continued to hold her close, stroking her back gently and holding the glass while she took a few sips of cold water.

The floor manager came over from his position behind the reservations desk and began to speak to Steve in a harried whisper. "Sir, the other patrons... If we could avoid a scene... If your friend is ill, perhaps we could offer a room?"

"Yes, I agree we should try to avoid publicity," Steve said curtly. He nodded briefly in Sally's direction. "Fortunately, Ms. Johansen is a guest in the hotel. We can go to her room until Mrs. Brookfield recovers. I'm sure you're as anxious to keep this incident out of the press as I am."

"What incident was that, sir? I didn't notice any incident. I see only that the young lady is feeling faint." The floor manager was standing straight once again. His voice and expression were both so bland that Megan had no idea if he was merely pretending ignorance or if he really hadn't seen the two men who accosted her.

Steve apparently had no such problem. "You have very adaptable eyesight," he said.

"Very adaptable," the manager agreed. "Flexibility is a requirement of my job, sir."

Steve looked down at Megan, who hadn't yet moved out of his arms. "You've stopped shaking," he said, the merest trace of tenderness in his voice. "Are you feeling okay now?"

"I'm fine." Megan finally recovered her voice. "Steve, let's just get out of here, please? All the people staring... I can't bear it."

His gaze flicked over her briefly, assessingly. "All right." He turned to Sally. "What's your room number?"

"Four twenty-seven." For once, even Sally sounded subdued.

Steve withdrew a credit card from his wallet and handed it to the manager. "Settle the bill for our lunch as fast as you can, will you? And send the card and the receipt up to Ms. Johansen's room."

"Certainly, sir. I'm glad the young lady is feeling better." The floor manager hurried away, and Steve turned to Sally.

"I should have asked you first," he said. "May we borrow your room for half an hour?"

"I don't mind if you borrow my room for the rest of the day, but I would like to know what's going on!"

"Let's get out of here before we attract any more interest than we already have." Steve kept his arm tightly around Megan's waist as he ushered her in the direction of the elevators. Her legs were no longer wobbling, but she convinced herself that she was still feeling too shaky to walk alone.

Sally had recovered her usual vivacity by the time they reached her room. "I want to know what happened," she demanded the minute the door was closed behind them. "I feel as though I've been taking part in a movie where everybody has a script except me. One minute we're all eating lunch like regular, normal people. The next minute Megan turns white as a sheet. She announces she's going to the ladies' room, and some reporter appears at our table. Steve tells the reporter to get lost and then starts prowling around the restaurant like a tiger scenting out his next night's dinner. And finally, just as I decided to abandon the last glass of champagne and join Steve on the prowl, he dashes behind a rhododendron and we find Megan practically fainting on the floor! Do you think you could clue me in on what's been happening?"

"I wish I knew," Steve said, his voice almost as grim as his expression. He walked away from Megan and stood by the telephone, his hand poised over the dial. "What happened, Megan?"

Refuge In His Arms 97

She hugged her arms around her body. She felt cold now that Steve was no longer holding her. "When I came out of the ladies' room those two men insisted on speaking to me. I tried to get away, but they grabbed hold of me and stopped me from walking away."

Steve waited for a moment, but when she said nothing more he prompted her impatiently. "And then what happened, Megan?"

"N—nothing much, I guess. They said they wanted to ask me some questions. They wouldn't let me go when I refused to answer." She saw the coolness of disbelief in Steve's eyes, and her own gaze dropped. "They were just persistent reporters, I guess. It's nothing to make such a big fuss about."

She didn't understand herself why she chose to make light of the incident, to pretend the men were journalists when they had specifically said they were not. Surely even Steve couldn't blame her because two total strangers had accosted her. But then, she wondered, if he wasn't angry, why was he looking at her so coldly? She hated it when he looked at her that way.

"Why didn't you call for help?" he asked curtly.

"Because..." She hesitated. She could hardly say she was afraid the men had guns. No reporter in England carried a gun; it was against the law. "Because I was scared," she said finally. "I panicked, and I guess I didn't behave very logically."

He was silent, and she knew he hadn't believed a word she said. She wished she could start the conversation over again and tell him the truth, but he and Sally would both think she was crazy—or a congenital liar—if she changed her story now. Before she met Jeffrey, she could hardly remember an occasion when she had told a lie, but for the past few days it seemed as if she had spent half her waking hours inventing plausible excuses and lying explanations.

"What did the men look like?" Steve asked.

"Look like?" She repeated his question, shocked by the realization that she had almost no idea how to answer him. She had been so filled with panic that she had reaped only the vaguest impression of bulk and menace.

"I don't know," she said helplessly. "They were tall, I think, and sort of heavily built. Their hands seemed kind of fat."

"What color was their hair? Their eyes? Their complexion? About how old were they?"

"Sort of middle-aged, I guess. Only one of them spoke, and he had a gold tooth." She shrugged, embarrassed by the inadequacy of her description. "I really don't remember what they looked like, Steve. I was trying to get away from them. I simply didn't notice their appearance!"

Steve made no further comment, although even Sally appeared a little surprised that she couldn't do better. "You're normally so observant, Meg," she murmured.

Steve's mouth tightened, and he picked up the phone. "Megan and I are going to have to leave in a couple of minutes, Sally. I'm sorry to cut our visit short, but you can see that Megan needs protection right at the moment, and I can't give it to her here."

"Yes." Sally glanced at Steve, a new awareness in her eyes. "You're a policeman, aren't you?"

"Sort of," he replied. "Do you mind if I use your phone for a local call?"

"Be my guest."

A bellhop arrived with Steve's credit card while he

was placing the call. Sally and Megan made no attempt to talk to each other when the bellhop had gone. They both eavesdropped shamelessly on Steve's call, but learned little. He identified himself by name and number, and thereafter his end of the conversation consisted of nothing more than the occasional yes or no. His facial expression never changed by so much as the flicker of an eyelash or the twitch of a muscle. His final words were no more informative than the sparse dialogue that had gone before.

"I see. Thank you for filling me in. I'm going to take Mrs. Brookfield home now. I'll file my report tonight."

He hung up the phone and turned to smile at Sally. "As you heard, we're going to leave, Sally. But I certainly enjoyed meeting you."

She smiled back at him. "I hope you realize you've ruined my vacation. You two have plunged me into the middle of a mystery, and I'm just about ready to die of curiosity!"

There was a hint of bleakness to Steve's smile. "I'm afraid it all sounds much more exciting than it really is. Most police work turns out to be nothing but routine investigation and mounds of paperwork in the end."

Megan gave her friend a quick, parting hug. "It's been so good to see you, Sally. I've missed you."

"Yes, I can see it's still not safe to let you go out alone. I hope you've learned your lesson. Next time don't get married until I give the guy my official seal of approval."

Megan managed a shaky laugh. "I won't. I promise."

Steve glanced impatiently at his watch. "Time to leave, Megan. The traffic will already be horrendous. If we wait any longer, it will be impossible."

He said nothing more to her until they were in the car, driving north across London toward Cambridge. He waited until they were halted at a traffic light; then he leaned back in his seat and looked at her intently.

"Okay," he said. "Now I'd like to know the truth. What did those two Soviet agents say to you?"

Chapter Seven

SHE SAT IN stunned silence for several seconds. Until Steve spoke the actual words, she hadn't allowed herself to accept the fact that the men who accosted her in the restaurant had really been spies. Even now, the thought seemed absurd. She was a perfectly ordinary person, or at least she had been until a few days ago, and ordinary people didn't get approached and questioned by foreign spies.

"How do you know they were Soviet agents?" she asked. "They looked like businessmen to me."

"Did they? I thought you didn't see them clearly enough to judge."

"Well, it's true I never saw them clearly, but they didn't look like Communist spies, for heaven's sake!"

"How do you expect Communist agents to look, Megan? Believe it or not, they don't walk around wearing astrakhan hats and speaking Russian. Of course those two men were agents. I can identify KGB operatives with one eye closed. It's one of the things I've been trained to do."

"All right, so you're a genius at your job! Good for you!" She drew a deep breath. "So maybe they were Soviet agents. Why are you mad at *me?* I didn't ask to be grabbed by two hulking great KGB men, you know."

"Didn't you?" The blue of Steve's eyes took on the hard, brilliant sheen of polished steel. "You were in a crowded restaurant, but you never once called out for help. Even when you saw me only a few yards away, you didn't so much as whisper my name. You collapsed in my arms—very convincingly, I might add—and while I was playing ministering angel, the two KGB men calmly walked out of the restaurant. And then, surprise, surprise! As soon as they were safely out of sight, you recovered from your fainting fit."

"I was frightened," she said despairingly. "Haven't you ever heard of people being paralyzed with fear? For God's sake, Steve, I'm not used to being physically attacked."

His mouth compressed into a hard, straight line. "You have to admit it's a startling coincidence that the very first time you're away from the cottage, two Soviet agents manage to make contact with you."

"Yes, but it *was* just a coincidence, I promise you. Perhaps they were following us. Perhaps they followed your car." Megan placed her hand on his arm in an unconscious gesture of appeal. "I should have told you

Refuge In His Arms 103

what they said to me, not tried to cover it up, but I know you don't trust me, and I didn't want to say anything that might make you more suspicious." She realized her hand was still resting on his arm, and she quickly drew it away.

"Those men just about scared me witless, Steve," she murmured, not looking at him. "I'm sure they were carrying guns, and they said... they said they had a message for me from Jeffrey. He wants me to join him in Moscow." The memory of those awful few minutes came back with vivid, heart-stopping clarity, and she gave a tight, nervous laugh. "Whether you believe me or not, I can assure you I don't want to have anything more to do with Jeffrey, not ever again. You don't know what it was like, those few weeks living with him..."

There was silence in the car as her voice died away. When Steve spoke again, his tone was crisp, business-like.

"Whether or not you're telling the truth is almost irrelevant. After today's incident at the restaurant, we have a responsibility to get you away somewhere safe. Either you're an innocent victim in all this, in which case you deserve protection. Or else you know a great deal more than you pretend, in which case it's my job to see that you don't make MI 6 and the CIA look like a bunch of incompetents. With all the attention the media have given you, it would be impossible to keep your disappearance a secret. And if you eventually turned up in Moscow, it would be a major propanganda success for the Communists."

Megan was filled with a dire sense of foreboding. "When you say you have to get me away somewhere safe, what do you mean? Are you about to throw me in jail?"

The austerity of his expression suddenly relaxed into a faint smile. "Nothing like that at all, I promise you. Almost every government has a few places dotted around the countryside that are safe from prying eyes and ears. They're usually located someplace where reporters and the general public aren't likely to come across them by accident. I'm going to make arrangements to take you to one of these safe houses, as they're called."

"I see." She looked out of the car window. "You say you're going to make the arrangements. Do you mean you will take me to this safe house?"

"I might." There was a momentary pause. "Do you object to the idea?"

"No," she said quietly, surprising herself with the simple truth of her answer. "I don't object. I think I feel... safer... with you around."

"Thank you. That's quite a compliment."

There was no mockery, no sarcasm in his voice. She stopped staring out of the car window and forced herself to look in his direction. His profile was as breathtakingly handsome as every other view of him. She swallowed hard, speaking quickly before she could lose her nerve. "Steve, if we're going to be spending so much time together, don't you think maybe we should forget our differences and just try to be friends?"

He halted the car at an intersection and turned to look at her again, his gaze resting on her mouth for a long, silent moment. "We could try," he said and immediately switched his attention back to the congested traffic.

She was piqued by the apparent coolness of his response. "You sound as if liking me is a superhuman task."

This time his eyes didn't leave the road ahead of them. "I think it might be," he said.

The traffic was heavy throughout the drive home, and it was early evening when they arrived back at Megan's cottage. They found the entrance guarded by a single uniformed police officer who was standing outside the garden gate trying not to look bored. Apart from a young boy on a bicycle, the street in front of the cottage was deserted.

Steve greeted the policeman. "Had a busy day, officer?"

"Not much to do at all, sir. Very quiet it's been since lunchtime."

"Two days ago there were fifty reporters here!" Megan exclaimed.

"Fame is fleeting in the age of television," Steve said dryly. "With any luck, a week from now there won't be a journalist left in the world who wants to interview you."

Although he had obviously recognized them, the police officer inspected their identification before allowing them into the house. Steve went straight to the phone and, after almost an hour of calling, returned to the living room and told Megan that everything was arranged for their departure. A small cottage in the most remote section of Montgomeryshire, in Wales, was being prepared for them. It would be ready the next day.

"Why don't you put a few basic necessities into a suitcase, while I make us something to eat," Steve said. "You only need to take personal items, no household supplies. The cottage is fully furnished, and the kitchen cupboards will be stocked with provisions."

Megan agreed and went upstairs. Her drawers and closets were so neatly organized that it didn't take more than a few minutes to pack. Looking out of the bedroom window, she could see that a fine drizzle of rain had begun, and the interior of the cottage felt a little chilly. She changed into a pair of slacks and a thin sweater before going back downstairs. After her years in Washington, D.C., she had found it hard to adjust to the cool dampness of the English summer.

When she returned to the kitchen, she found Steve stirring something in a big pot on the stove. He had taken off his jacket and tie and rolled up his shirtsleeves, displaying darkly tanned, muscular forearms and the strong, smooth column of his throat. He had found one of Megan's pink polka-dotted aprons and was wearing it tied around his waist with a slightly off-center bow. The apron somehow seemed to emphasize the uncompromising masculinity of his physique and the disciplined fitness of his body.

He became aware of her presence in the kitchen and straightened from his task at the stove, smiling as he greeted her. "Hi! You finished your packing quickly. Supper will be another couple of minutes yet."

"It doesn't take long to throw a few T-shirts and some toilet articles into a bag. Can I do anything to help with the meal?"

"It's all under control."

"You certainly look very well organized. Have you done a lot of cooking?"

"I'll take all the compliments I can get, but I feel obligated to point out that it's hard to look disorganized heating a can of mushroom soup!"

"I don't believe a can of soup can smell this good!"

Steve added a hefty measure of sherry to the contents of the pot, then grinned at her disarmingly. "Well, I doctored it up a little. There was some cream in the refrigerator, and I found a few herbs. The sherry helps, too. Or maybe you smell the bread. There was a loaf of French bread in the freezer, and I put it in the oven to warm. Perhaps you could check to see if it's hot?"

A few minutes later he pronounced everything ready. They arranged their bowls of soup and slices of crusty, buttered break on two wooden trays and carried their meal into the living room to eat while they watched an old Alfred Hitchcock movie on television.

They didn't talk much, but Megan felt some of the strain of the past few days slipping away as they swapped occasional laughing comments about the film. Halfway through the movie she kicked off her shoes and curled up on the sofa. Steve lounged in the armchair near her, his long legs stretched out, his body totally relaxed. She was aware of a subtle feeling of warmth and companionship every time she glanced in his direction. It must be the hot soup that was making her feel so relaxed and comfortable, she thought. Steve's concoction had tasted more like sherry lightly flavored with mushroom soup than the other way around. She smiled at the thought, and Steve looked at her quizzically.

"A bird is about to peck out the heroine's eyes and you're *smiling?* I hadn't realized I was watching television with a sadist."

She laughed. "I've never been able to take this story seriously, although most of Hitchcock's movies have me jumping at my own shadow."

The movie rolled to its predictably horrendous climax just as the front doorbell rang.

"I'll get that," Steve said.

Megan switched off the television set and followed him into the tiny hall. A uniformed policeman was talking to Steve. "I've brought your luggage, sir," he said. "It was sent down from London as you requested."

"Thanks for bringing it around, officer, I appreciate the service. I know how much extra work we've caused you all over the past week."

"No trouble at all, sir. We were pleased to help out. I'm going off duty now, so I'll say good night." He nodded politely to Megan. "Good night to you, Mrs. Brookfield. There shouldn't be any problems tonight; the men on the beat will be keeping a sharp lookout for any troublemakers."

When the policeman had gone, Steve locked and bolted the front door. He and Megan remained in the hallway, although neither of them spoke. The tension that had been absent all evening seemed inexplicably to have returned in full force. Megan ran her tongue over dry lips, aware that Steve's gaze followed the movement.

"I . . . I didn't see a policeman on duty at the front gate," she said.

"No. He left several hours ago. The local police force is too short of men to keep somebody on guard here any longer."

"Oh." Megan sensed the indefinable restraint in Steve's manner and couldn't guess at its cause. His hair was slightly tousled where he had been resting his head against the high back of the chair, and she had to resist an almost overwhelming urge to reach out and smooth the thick strands away from his forehead. She glanced at her watch without even seeing the numbers of its face, then cleared her throat nervously.

"Well, it's getting late, Steve. Since we're making an early start tomorrow, I think I'll go to bed. By the way, there's no need for you to spend the night on the sofa. There's a spare bedroom upstairs, and the bed is already made up. You may as well sleep in comfort."

Steve spoke very softly. "I have to sleep in your room tonight, Megan, but you already know that, don't you?"

"No! How could I know anything so crazy?" Her reply was little more than a whisper because she had to fight back a sudden, unnerving vision of Steve Callahan sleeping in her bed. The image was unsettling—she couldn't imagine why it had to come to her—and when she spoke again, her tone was sharper than she had intended. "I can't think of a single reason why you need to spend the night in my room. You've boasted what a light sleeper you are. Why can't you sleep in the spare bedroom?"

"Because there are no policemen guarding the outside of the cottage. Because two men tried to kidnap you today. Because, although I'm a light sleeper, I'm not superman, and I can't be certain to wake when I should. You'll be safer if I'm in your room, Megan."

"Will I?"

"Yes." His voice was flat. "I'm here to protect you, not for any other reason."

She turned away, aware of a strange, trembling ache lodged somewhere in the pit of her stomach. She ignored the feeling, covering it up with a flash of anger. There was no way she would allow Steve to spend the night in her room, but she was wise enough not to defy him openly.

"I'm going to take a shower before I go to bed," she

said abruptly. "You'll find a sleeping bag on the top shelf of the hall closet. Take a pillow from the spare bedroom if you want it."

"Thanks." His voice was as abrupt as hers. "I still have quite a few things to do. You'll probably be asleep before I come upstairs."

"Probably. Good night."

She showered quickly, then hurried back into her bedroom, hugging her terry-cloth robe tightly around her still-damp body. Fortunately, Steve was nowhere in sight. He had already unrolled the sleeping bag in a corner of the room and placed a pillow at its head.

Megan smiled with grim satisfaction as she closed the door of her room and quietly turned the heavy, old-fashioned lock. For good measure, she slipped the equally old-fashioned iron bolt into place. Agent Callahan was about to discover that she wasn't easily manipulated and that she wouldn't submit meekly to all his ridiculous orders. He would need an ax to get into her room tonight, she thought gleefully.

She hung the robe neatly on a hook behind the bedroom door and pulled on a red and white striped nightshirt. She returned to her bed and sat on it cross-legged, flipping through the pages of a magazine.

She waited almost thirty minutes before she heard Steve's firm, quick steps coming up the wooden stairs. Quickly she switched off the bedside lamp, plunging the room into darkness. She heard the sound of the bathroom door opening, followed by several minutes of silence. The walls of the old cottage were thick and virtually soundproof. She hugged her knees, anticipating her moment of triumph with increasing pleasure.

Refuge In His Arms   111

The wooden floor creaked again as Steve walked quietly along the corridor from the bathroom. He paused outside her door and gently turned the handle, evidently trying not to make too much noise in case she was already asleep. Megan stifled a giggle. He tried again, less gently, but with equal lack of success, and this time she couldn't restrain a childish gurgle of triumph.

"Having problems, Agent Callahan?" she asked sweetly.

Unfortunately Steve didn't lose his temper and bang angrily on the door. Just once, she thought, it would be exciting to see what he was like when he lost his veneer of rigid self-control. She wondered if anybody had ever seen him relax the iron guard he kept over his emotions. She wondered what he would be like when he made love... As soon as the thought came into her mind, she pushed it away, angry at its irrelevance.

Far from losing his temper, he didn't even bother to rattle the door handle again. He knocked sharply, authoritatively, just once.

"Megan," he said. "Will you please open this door?"

"No. Go away. I don't want you in here. I'm entitled to *some* privacy."

"Megan, for your own safety I need to be in that room tonight."

"Sure, I've heard it all before. The U.S. government flew you and three thousand ducklings over here especially to protect me. After a few days of your services, however, I've decided I'd prefer the ducklings."

"Tomorrow I'll see if I can get them shipped in. Tonight, you'll have to make do with me." His voice softened, and she could almost see the smile that warmed his eyes. "Open the door, Meg, please?"

Nobody called her Meg except Sally and, for some reason, the nickname sounded almost caressing when he spoke it. She slid angrily down in the bed, pulling the covers up to her chin. "I'm going to sleep, *Agent Callahan*. Would you please stop pounding on that door?"

She had no idea what reaction she had anticipated from Steve. Perhaps, in her heart of hearts, she had almost expected him to find an ax and break down the door. Whatever she had expected, however, it certainly hadn't been total silence. After less than a minute, she heard his footsteps retreating down the stairs. Although she was glad she had won the minor battle, she admitted to herself that, in some obscure way, she was disappointed. Her victory tasted mysteriously flat.

Having won the right to sleep alone, she had nothing left to do except concentrate on falling asleep. Her mind was teeming with unresolved problems, but she was physically exhausted after several nights of disturbed rest, and she eventually drifted off into a dream-filled slumber.

She wasn't sure precisely what tiny noise jerked her back into wakefulness. She sat up in bed, her throat dry and her heart pounding. Now that she was fully awake, she heard another noise: the faint chink of metal scraping against metal, followed by the unmistakable sound of her sash window being opened.

Fear was like a mist that surrounded her, choking off her power to breathe. She stared through the semidarkness of the room and saw the menacing black shadow of a man outlined against the filmy bedroom curtains. It required an incredible effort of will to fight off the paralyzing effects of her fear. She screamed at the top of her lungs.

Refuge In His Arms

"Steve, Steve! For God's sake come quickly!"

She flung herself out of bed and dashed to the bedroom door, fumbling with the heavy bolt. The metal was old, and the lock was stiff, and fear made her fingers clumsy. She hadn't even succeeded in drawing back the bolt when she was seized in a grip like steel bars. She stopped screaming and began to fight with desperate, silent determination.

"Damn it, Megan, will you stop kicking long enough to turn around and see who you're attacking?"

She whirled around in his arms and found herself face to face with Steve. Her fear vanished, and fury boiled over to take its place. She launched herself at him with all the force of her body weight, pounding on his chest until she was exhausted. For all the discomfort her blows seemed to cause him, she might as well have conserved her energy. Her anger gradually drained away in the face of his passive resistance, and she sank wearily onto the bed.

"How could you, Steve?" she asked. "How could you do something so cruel?"

"Very easily," he replied grimly. "And that was the whole point of the exercise."

He sat down on the bed next to her, pulling her into his arms and brushing the remains of a tear away with his thumb. "Megan, I'm sorry, but I had to show you how vulnerable you are if you lock yourself alone in this room. There's a huge apple tree outside the window that any agile six-year-old could climb. And the locks of those window sashes come undone with a pocket knife."

"Nobody's going to want to climb into my bedroom. Except you."

"You didn't think anybody was going to grab you

when you met your friend for lunch."

She could think of no reasonable answer to that remark, so she remained silent.

"Megan, look at me, please. I didn't want to frighten you, but I had to get into your room. You saw how stiff those locks were. You couldn't open the door when you wanted to. You understand now how easily you could be trapped in here."

When she didn't respond, he put his hand gently beneath her chin and tilted her face upward. "Am I forgiven, Meg?"

His eyes seemed unexpectedly tender in the dimness of the bedroom, his expression hesitant, almost questioning.

She was afraid to answer his silent question, so she closed her eyes. "Your clothes are wet," she said, trying to find some way to steer the conversation onto neutral ground. "You ought to change them."

"It's raining heavily, but I'm not cold." He made no attempt to get up from the bed nor did he remove his dark sweater, despite the obvious patches of damp on the shoulders.

"You'll catch a chill," she murmured. "And then you'll have to stay in bed drinking hot lemon tea when you should be out catching spies."

"I'll take the risk," he said huskily. "Megan, why are we talking about wet clothes for heaven's sake? That's got absolutely nothing to do with what either of us is thinking."

Before she could find an adequate answer, he reached out and touched the tip of his finger to her lips. "Shall I tell you what I'm really thinking?" he asked softly.

"I'm thinking you have the most beautiful mouth I've ever seen. I'm thinking that I very badly want to kiss you."

A sharp thrill of pleasure coursed through her at his words, but she fought to deny it. She reminded herself that Steve was a federal agent and that, as far as she was concerned, he was little better than her jailer. But somehow the reminder seemed unimportant in comparison with the way he could make her feel.

Hesitantly she stretched out her hand and traced the outline of his mouth with her thumb. His lips felt firm and cool beneath her fingers, but she noticed that his cheeks were darkened with a flush of color. When her thumb finally halted its exploration at the corner of his mouth, he turned his face toward her hand and pressed a single hard kiss against the pulse beating in her wrist.

The shock of pleasure she felt was so intense that she shivered, but she tried to conceal her reaction, even from herself.

"Steve, we can't do this," she said, although he hadn't spoken, and she wasn't at all sure precisely what it was they couldn't do. "This is insane. It's crazy." She gave a tiny gasp of laughter. "It's probably even illegal."

"Do you think I don't know that?" His words were no more than a harsh murmur against the palm of her hand, but Megan found the whisper of his breath across her skin the most erotic sensation she had ever experienced. For years she had told herself that sexual passion was something for other women, not for her. Passion made women vulnerable, and she was determined never to allow herself to be vulnerable to any man. She had learned to live with parental rejection. She could even learn to accept Jeffrey's betrayal because she had only liked him, never loved him. But she didn't think she could learn to live with rejection from a man she had allowed herself to love.

"For once in my life I want to forget the rules," Steve said. "I don't want to think or to rationalize. I just want to feel."

His head bent slowly, inexorably toward her mouth. When their lips finally met, the contact was electrifying. The ache in Megan's womb coiled into a tight spiral of need as he brushed his lips caressingly over hers, teasing and tempting with the lightness of his touch until she ached to feel the hard, aggressive thrust of his tongue inside her mouth. She had never known, until tonight, that a woman's entire body could burn with the need to be kissed. She parted her lips, and her mouth moved hungrily beneath his, pleading for satisfaction. She felt her body tremble with desire, a desire that increased when she saw Steve's eyes grow dark and slumberous with passion.

She leaned back against the pillows, her seductive movements urging him to lie across her body with a deliberate provocation she had never before practiced and still only half understood.

Heavy with desire, Steve's eyes roamed over her body. Then with a sudden, muffled exclamation, he lay down beside her. When he kissed her again, his restraint had vanished. His tongue sought out the deepest recesses of her mouth with a tumultuous, thrusting urgency. At the same time, his hands reached for the buttons of her nightshirt, and she felt the coolness of the night air ripple over her bare breasts. But as soon as his hands touched her

Refuge In His Arms 117

skin, the coolness changed to a burning, flaming heat.

She closed her eyes, reaching out blindly to twist her fingers into his hair, stroking her thumbs along his jaw in a deliberately erotic rhythm. The feel of his mouth against her breast was driving her beyond the point of reason. With a physical urgency that she had never before experienced, she wanted to feel his body lying naked against her own. She wanted to surrender herself to the sweet and terrifying threat of his possession.

She unwound her hands from his hair and groped for the waistband of his thick, cable-knit sweater, pulling it away from his jeans with impatient, searching fingers. She discovered that he was wearing nothing beneath the heavy sweater and, as she tugged it up toward his shoulders, she reveled in the smooth, firm feel of his skin and the ripple of his muscles under her fingers.

It only took her a couple of seconds to push his sweater as far as his rib cage, and then her mindless pleasure came to an end, for there, somewhere around the level of his upper ribs, high under his left arm, she felt the leather gun holster.

When she realized what she was touching, her brain blanked out with shock. Her hands, however, had developed a will of their own, and they continued to move upward until her fingers closed around the rough, textured surface of the gun butt. The fact that she was on the point of making love to a man who didn't trust her enough to remove his gun holster pierced the numbness of her brain, but then her thought processes froze solid, her mind and body equally incapable of action.

The silence in the bedroom seemed to stretch out forever. Steve sat up slowly, reaching for her hands and removing them with almost impersonal efficiency. After an eternity of time. Megan discovered she had regained her power of speech.

"You have a gun," she said.

Steve turned away so that she could no longer see his face. "Of course I have a gun." he said. "I'm an agent on active duty."

"Very active," she said with a sarcasm that she hoped might mask her bitter sense of loss. "I should have remembered that seducing enemy agents was your specialty."

He turned to look at her, his gaze resting thoughtfully on the open front of her nightshirt, which she had forgotten to button. The pale swell of her breasts was clearly visible in the moonlight. Despite the shadowy darkness of the bedroom, she had the impression that his mouth hardened into bleakness. "Are you an enemy agent, Megan?" he asked.

She wanted to cry. She wanted to crawl under the bedclothes. She wanted to throw herself into his arms and make love to him until there was no space left in their minds for reason or doubt or suspicion. She drew a hand wearily across her eyes.

"I'm going to sleep," she said, pulling the bedcovers up to her chin.

Steve said nothing. He ripped off his sweater and tossed it into a corner of the room. An errant beam of moonlight struck against the metal surface of his gun, causing it to gleam with a dull, gray sheen. He didn't unclip the holster or remove the gun. He bent down to take off his shoes, then straightened to unzip his jeans. Megan looked hurriedly away.

When she felt sure it was safe to look at him again,

she saw that Steve was already inside the sleeping bag.

The night seemed virtually endless to Megan, and her only minor consolation was the certain knowledge that Steve, lying unnaturally still and silent in his sleeping bag, slept no more than she did.

Chapter Eight

SHE MUST HAVE fallen asleep some time before dawn, because the last thing she remembered was darkness. When she woke up the sun was shining, and Steve had already left her room. He had cleared away his sleeping bag and pillow and had picked up his discarded clothes.

She glanced at the clock on the nightstand. It was only six-thirty, but the drive could easily take more than four hours if they ran into heavy traffic. She showered and dressed quickly in jeans, a white cotton blouse, and a soft green sweater. After almost two years in England she was no longer deceived by the morning sun. By noon it could well be raining, and, even if the day remained dry, the temperature was unlikely to go much above seventy.

When she entered the kitchen, she found Steve sitting at the table drinking coffee. He was wearing sweat pants and a faded T-shirt, which suggested he might have been exercising. If he had, the exercises hadn't raised much sweat. He looked as fresh and alert as if he had spent eight hours deeply asleep in a comfortable bed, and she realized that his physical fitness went far beyond an attractive tan and a few sleek muscles.

She was disconcerted to find that she was still so aware of his physical attractions. She had assumed that, after the debacle of the previous night, she would find the sight of his body repellent. In fact, the opposite was true. Knowing something of the physique beneath the thin cotton shirt and faded pants, she was hard put to resist the urge to move closer to him.

When she finally realized how long they had been staring at each other, she spoke hurriedly to fill a silence that was rapidly becoming fraught with tension. "I'm sorry if I overslept. I hope I haven't kept you waiting."

"No problem. I'm glad you slept well." If there was sarcasm in his words, she couldn't hear it. "I've cleared all the perishable items out of the refrigerator, and I've made arrangements for your mail to be picked up."

"How efficient. Thank you."

He looked at her sharply, then stood up and carried his empty mug to the sink. "If you want to make yourself breakfast, the coffee's still hot. I'll change while you're eating. I'd like to miss the morning rush hour out of Cambridge if we can."

"I'll be ready by the time you come downstairs," she said.

* * *

It took them a little over an hour to drive to Leicester, a town in the Midland region of England that was directly on their route into Wales. Instead of following the signs for Wales, however, Steve took the Leicester City exit from the motorway and drove quickly to a police station in the town center. He parked their gray Rover in the station yard and ushered Megan inside.

As soon as he showed his identification, they were taken through the building into a back parking lot and given the keys to a blue Ford Fiesta, one of the most common cars on British roads. Steve was also handed a small cardboard carton, completely closed with strapping tape and with the British Crown Seal affixed on each corner. Within five minutes of their arrival, they were driving out of the police station in their new car.

"What on earth was all that about?" Megan asked when they were once again back on the motorway, heading for Wales.

He shrugged. "A precaution in case we were being followed. A couple of plainclothes cops—the woman looks a bit like you—are going to drive the Rover north toward Nottingham and then double back to Leicester. There's no point in taking you to Wales and bringing an unwanted escort with us."

Megan shook her head in bewilderment "Honestly, Steve, none of this seems real to me. I can't believe anybody would bother to follow us."

"They probably won't. Just forget about it. It's my responsibility to see that nothing happens to you."

"I'm not your responsibility," she said quickly. "I'm not anybody's responsibility. I'm quite capable of taking care of myself. I've been doing it for years."

"All of us can use the occasional helping hand," he

said quietly. "It isn't a crime to admit that you might need somebody's support, Megan."

She turned away and stared out of the window. "Oh, look! It's only another thirteen miles to the Welsh border," she said brightly. "We've made good time."

"Yes, I noticed. I also noticed that you changed the subject again."

Shortly before noon they arrived at the cottage. It was set in about an acre of roughly cut grass, situated at the end of a rutted, unpaved country lane. The property was surrounded by a mellowed stone wall that had honeysuckle and wild roses growing profusely over it. On one side the cottage was screened by hills that seemed to rise almost directly out of the back yard. On the other side it was bounded by a deep, fast-flowing stream that Steve identified from his map as a tributary of the River Severn. There were no other houses in sight, and the closest town—several miles away—was a small tourist center built around the medieval Powys Castle.

Megan got out of the car and waited while Steve locked the doors and pocketed the ignition key. She breathed in a deep gulp of air, fresh from the nearby mountains, and felt the midday sun warm her face. The quiet and the solitude were so intense as to be almost tangible. She understood at once why the government considered the cottage such a safe retreat, but her own overwhelming impression was simply that it was one of the most perfect vacation spots she had ever seen.

They picked up their luggage and walked together to the front door. The windows, Megan noticed, were all heavily barred, which destroyed some of the vacation-home image. She waited while Steve broke open the sealed carton he had been given at the Leicester police station and removed a set of three keys. He needed to use all three in order to open the door.

The cottage was tiny. The front door opened straight into the living room, and a door at the other end of the living room opened straight into the kitchen. If there had once been a back door, it had been bricked over when the cottage was modernized. There was no way into the cottage except from the front entrance. A narrow wooden staircase, uncarpeted, led upstairs to the only bedroom (twin beds, Megan noted thankfully) and a modern bathroom. She turned on the hot water faucet, relieved to find that it immediately gushed out boiling hot water.

Steve grinned approvingly at the curl of steam, then walked back into the bedroom and dumped his weekend bag onto one of the beds. "This is a pretty nice place. Now if I'd only brought my fishing tackle, I could have a real vacation! That river looks as if the trout are just about jumping out onto the banks."

"Thank heaven you don't have fishing tackle; that's all I can say."

"Don't you like fishing?"

"Not much. But what I really hate is having to eat the fish once it's caught. All the fishermen I know insist on cooking the wretched creatures over a wood fire, with their heads on, and then you get served this platter of smoky broiled trout with two glassy gray eyes staring reproachfully up at you."

He laughed. "If you can't stand nature in the raw, the food provided here should suit you just fine. It's all either canned or freeze-dried, and the stuff inside the package doesn't look much like anything you've ever seen growing or moving."

"Sounds great. Just my kind of provisions. If you like, I'll volunteer to make us lunch."

He glanced out of the bedroom window. The sun was striking the hilltops, making them shimmer with a golden haze of brightness. "Could you make sandwiches, do you think? I'd love to explore those hills, and we could take a picnic."

She didn't stop to analyze the intense pleasure she felt at his suggestion. "Yes, let's do that. It may never be sunny again while we're here, so we ought to take this chance to explore a little."

They followed a path alongside the river back toward the hills until the river and the path diverged. Steve had a compass with him, but, in fact, it was impossible to lose their way provided they didn't wander far from the beaten track.

The path was well worn, but they met absolutely nobody, and Steve suggested they might be walking along an unused sheep trail. Montgomeryshire had been a center for the medieval woolen trade, and Welshpool, the largest town in the county, had been famous for its production of flannel cloth. Megan realized that the hills which now seemed so deserted must once have been dotted with grazing sheep.

The path led consistently upward after it left the banks of the river, but it wasn't steep, and about halfway up the hill it widened into a natural resting place. Four large, flat boulders made ideal seats, and the view over the river valley was spectacular.

"Shall we stop here?" Steve suggested. "It looks like a good place to eat lunch."

"Anywhere would look terrific to me at the moment. I'm starving."

They each carried a small pack containing a thermos of fruit juice and a couple of sandwiches. Megan sat down on one of the sun-warmed rocks, resting her back against the grass-covered hillside. The bread had been frozen when she made the sandwiches, but it had defrosted during their walk and now, as far as she was concerned, tasted absolutely delicious.

They munched in satisfied silence for a minute or two. Then Steve pulled apart his slices of bread and peered at the grayish filling. "Er... precisely what's in these sandwiches?" he asked.

She grinned. "Sardines and canned relish. I think it tastes pretty good. How about you?"

"'Unusual' is the word that springs to mind."

This time she laughed aloud. "You must agree the fruit juice is fantastic."

"Yes." He sighed contentedly and took another sip from his plastic cup. "I can't believe I'm eating sardines and canned relish—and enjoying it! I'd forgotten how good everything tastes when you eat it outdoors. I didn't have much time for picnicking while I was living in Luxembourg."

She ate the last crumb of her sandwich, then clasped her hands behind her head and squinted up at the sky. It had been a long time since she last felt so pleasurably relaxed. "What do you actually do, Steve? I mean, I know you work for the CIA, but what were you doing while you lived in Luxembourg?"

"Trying to stop American high-technology products from getting shipped to the Communist bloc countries.

People can make a great deal of money selling American equipment to Eastern Europe, but most high-technology products require an export license from the U.S. government, so there's an illegal trade in licenses. You'd be amazed at the lengths people will go to get around the government's regulations. Communist countries set up phony companies in Western Europe with a legitimate business as cover. Luxembourg shares international borders with Belgium, Germany, and France, so it's a favorite spot for headquartering that sort of company."

"How did you manage to stop the shipments? Did you ride out in the middle of the night and physically heave the crates of equipment off the planes, or something?"

He laughed, crumpling up the foil from his sandwiches and returning it to his pack. "Hell, no! I just let it be known in various quarters that I was very willing to act as front man for any companies that Communist governments wanted to set up. In the past five years I've been president of more corporations than you could count."

"Wasn't it dangerous? I mean, wouldn't they have been mad if they found out what you were doing?"

"Probably," he said dryly. "But I took damn good care not to let them find out."

"And now? Why did you leave Luxembourg?"

A shadow crossed his face. "My cover was blown," he said. "I trusted somebody I shouldn't have trusted, and my boss hauled me back to Washington on the first plane out of the city."

"I'm sorry." She bit her lip, thinking of Jeffrey. "It's ... hard when somebody you trust betrays you." He didn't answer, and she said, "What will happen to you now, Steve?"

"Oh, I'm in luck. I've been promoted. When my assignment in England is finished, I'll be on my way back to a desk job in Washington, D.C. I get my own office, a fancy carpet, a secretary all to myself, and a salary increase as well."

"You don't sound too thrilled about the promotion."

"I'm not interested in spending my time writing inter-office memos for circulation around the in-trays of CIA headquarters," he said curtly.

"Then make sure you say something important, and the memo will go straight to the top."

The shadow disappeared from his eyes, and his mouth relaxed into a grin. He slid off his perch on the rock and looked at her ruefully. "Why is good advice always so annoying, I wonder?"

He walked around a bend in the path without giving her time to answer and returned only seconds later. "The track leads straight up to the top of the hill, but I think it would be an easy climb down the other side of the hill back to the river. Do you want to try it?"

"How easy is easy?" Megan asked cautiously. "Keeping in mind that my definition of strenuous exercise is an hour of aerobic dance class."

"It's scarcely a climb at all, I promise. We have no climbing gear with us, so I wouldn't suggest it if the descent was much more than a steep walk. And we could cool off in the river once we get down."

It was the prospect of dunking her feet into cool, flowing water that convinced Megan to make the descent. Despite the bright sunshine, the temperature probably wasn't much more than seventy. But her long-sleeved shirt was sticking to her back after the two-hour walk, and her jeans were definitely too hot to be comfortable.

They were much less than a quarter of the way down when Megan realized that what Steve categorized as an easy walk, she categorized as an impossible climb. She was reasonbly fit, but clambering down the rock-strewn face of a steep hill challenged her skills to the limit. She was breathless, her limbs trembling with exhaustion, by the time they reached the river. She flopped down on the grassy bank, pulled off her shoes, yanked up her jeans, and wriggled her toes ecstatically in the cool, clear water.

When she had recovered enough energy to turn her head, she looked back at the hill they had just descended. "My God, it's a precipice!" she exclaimed as soon as she had breath to spare for speaking. "You made me climb down a precipice!"

Steve, who looked cool, lithe, and disgustingly full of energy, smiled at her tolerantly. "It did turn out to be a bit steeper than I'd expected," he said. "But it was worth it. Look, the river water here is deep enough for swimming."

"Terrific. Unfortunately nobody told me to bring a swimsuit."

"I don't mind one bit if you swim in the raw," he said, his voice husky with a hint of laughter. "In fact, I think we might both enjoy the experience."

His words caused a wave of heat to wash under her skin, but she forced herself to ignore it. She even managed to ignore the sweet, shivering weakness that invaded her limbs at the thought of swimming naked with him in the clear river water. She gave him a withering glance, then closed her eyes and lay back in the lush grass, resting her head on her arms and letting her legs sink knee-deep into the water "You're in luck, Steve. I'm too tired to hit you. I'm even too tired to feel mad at you."

"How can you be exhausted after a simple little stroll down a hillside? You must be shockingly out of condition."

She kept her eyes closed and turned her head pointedly away from the direction of his voice. "That remark isn't worth answering," she said with as much dignity as she could muster. "It's impolite, it's elitist, and it's probably sexist as well."

"But also truthful," he murmured.

She yawned widely. "Go flex a few muscles, Steve. I'm planning to take a nap."

A low chuckle of laughter was his only response, and the next sound she heard was the clean, sharp thunk of his shallow dive into the river. As soon as she was sure he wasn't looking at her, she opened her eyes and watched him slice through the water in a rapid crawl. He swam about twenty yards downstream before he flip-dived, turned, and raced back again.

He swam so many laps that Megan began to wonder what he was trying to prove to himself. He swam with a fierce, almost brutal concentration that carried him up and down the stretch of deep river at an incredible speed. She was sure, however, that he wasn't trying to impress her with his physical prowess; he took his fitness too much for granted for that.

She watched the tremendous power of his tanned shoulders as he shot through the fast-flowing water, and felt an unwelcome flash of awareness spark through her body. She immediately turned away and looked along the riverbank, but the change of view wasn't much help in controlling her wayward emotions. Steve's cutoffs and his shirt were resting in a neat pile at the water's edge, together with his lunch pack. A bump in the folds of the shirt hinted at the presence of the leather gun holster that probably lay beneath. The images of Steve's unclothed body that sprang into her mind were so vivid and so erotic that she rolled over onto her stomach and buried her face in her hands, as if by covering her eyes she could succeed in blacking out the seductive pictures her mind was producing.

She had been lying face down on the grass for about five minutes when she heard Steve climb out of the water and walk toward her, his footsteps partly muffled by the long grass. She lay still, pretending to be unaware of his approach, and suddenly a cascade of freezing cold water descended on the middle of her back.

She shot into a sitting position and whirled around. "Steve, you sadistic monster!" she breathed, pummeling his chest in mock fury. "I'll pay you back for that, you just wait!"

He knelt beside her, catching her wrists in one of his hands. When she saw the expression on his face, all the laughter drained out of her in a single quick gasp. Her body reacted to the passion in his eyes before her mind had a chance to say no, and she bent her head, brushing her cheek swiftly against his clenched fists.

She felt the faintest answering touch of his fingers against her face, but when he spoke, his voice was low, carefully controlled, as if he was afraid to reveal too much of what he was feeling. "You have a wild flower caught in your hair. I think it's a buttercup."

She took the flower from him, avoiding his gaze and avoiding the sight of his lean, tanned body clad only in dark-colored underpants. "I think...I think it's time for us to go, Steve." Her breathing was suddenly strained and nervous, and she tried unsuccessfully to give a casual laugh. "I guess this flower is just the tip of the problem. It'll probably take me hours to get rid of all the grass in my hair."

He ran his hand lightly over the dark, tumbled mass. "I'll help you brush it. But later, not now."

"No..." she whispered, terrified by the way her body was responding to his nearness. What was happening to her? She was supposed to be the sensible person in her family, the woman who understood that heartbreak and humiliation always followed in the wake of physical passion. She was supposed to be the woman who based all her relationships with men on affection and respect and shared interests. She was supposed to be the woman who despised the irrational, magnetic attraction of sexual desire.

"No," she said again with a hint of desperation in her voice. She knew she was denying her own feelings more than she was denying anything Steve had said. She tried to get up, but his hands grasped her shoulders and prevented her from moving.

"It's no good running away, Meg," he said quietly. "We can't run away from our own feelings. I've been doing that all day, and I've finally given up fighting the inevitable. There's no way I can convince myself that I don't want you. Climbing down a mountain didn't help, and the swim sure as hell didn't do a thing for me. I want to make love to you."

The husky timbre of his voice was intoxicating, making her blood race and her heart pound. The world around them seemed to be fading into a golden haze of warmth and sunlight, and yet, at the time, her senses had never seemed more fully alive. She could hear the faint buzz of an insect, but the sound seemed to come from far away, for her ears were filled by the sound of his voice, just as her eyes were filled by the sight of him.

He touched his fingertips to her throat, and she tipped her head backward, instinctively baring her throat to his caress. His mouth pressed against the pulse hammering in the hollow of her neck, and she knew in that instant that there was nothing in the world she wanted so much as to lie down in the grass and feel his cool, hard body pressed against hers and to hear his dark, smoky voice whispering words of endearment against her skin.

Some lingering shred of common sense kept her sitting upright. "Steve, we can't do this," she whispered. "There's your job... The CIA..."

"To hell with my job " he murmured harshly. "Megan, please let me love you." She twisted her head away, but he captured her face between his hands, and his eyes blazed as he looked down at her. She felt the sudden, quick shudder of his body. Then his eyes closed and he sought her mouth blindly, hungrily.

His lips caressed her, cool and firm and unexpectedly tender. For an endless moment she was aware of nothing save the touch of his mouth against hers and the slight pressure of his wet skin against her sun-warmed body. His fingers twined in the tangled thickness of her hair and stroked slowly across her shoulders, down to her breasts. His thumbs drew lightly across her nipples, and the golden haze that had surrounded her began to shimmer, leaving her dizzy with the need for his possession.

"Megan, you're so beautiful." His words were no more than a murmur, almost lost against her mouth. "You've been driving me insane ever since the morning I arrived at your house." His voice shook slightly when he spoke, and she saw that his eyes had darkened and his mouth had softened, revealing all the vulnerability normally hidden behind his hard, professional mask.

She murmured his name, her voice rising into a whispered question. He took her hand and guided it to his chest, then stroked it purposefully down his body. "You can feel what you've done to me, Megan," he said thickly. "Let me make you feel the same need I do." His hands cupped her breasts enticingly, and his thumbs gently teased her nipples, making them tingle with life beneath her thin cotton blouse.

She gave up her last, lingering pretense of resistance. "I already need you," she admitted. "Kiss me, Steve. Please..."

His head bent slowly toward her, and suddenly he was kissing her with savage, burning intensity. She opened her mouth on a gasp of pleasure. and his tongue made an immediate, violent invasion. Her blood pounded in her ears, and her breath raced crazily as she felt the hard, demanding thrust of his body against hers. She clung to him in helpless surrender, and only some tiny remnant of pride prevented her from begging him to take her quickly. She guessed how much control he was exercising over his actions, and some wanton part of her yearned to have the trembling ache of her need assuaged by the unrestrained fierceness of his passion.

Without breaking his kiss, he unbuttoned her blouse, pushing it caressingly from her shoulders. He unfastened the front clip of her bra with practiced ease, but she felt his fingers shake against her skin, and she was glad that her body had the power to arouse him so dramatically. She felt the cool rush of air across her breasts as he tossed the bra into the grass, then heard his breath exhale in a sudden, uneven outpouring. Her body was quivering by the time he pushed the zipper of her jeans slowly downward, his fingers brushing tantalizingly against her stomach. She tightened the clasp of her arms around his neck and arched her body closer to his, moving her hips restlessly against him until she felt the crisp hair of his chest prickle against her nipples and the heightened urgency of his desire against her thighs.

She moaned protestingly when he finally lifted his lips from hers, then shuddered in satisfaction as his mouth followed the path down her body already trailed by his fingers. Bemused by the intensity of her own feelings, she felt a faint shock of bewilderment when she realized that she was naked, her clothes all removed by Steve's expert, caressing hands.

His body was no longer cooled by river water when he lay beside her in the long grass. His back glistened with a thin sheen of sweat, and his high cheekbones were darkened with desire. His hand traced an erotic circle on her flat stomach, moving gradually lower until his fingers slipped between her legs and teased them open. Her body made an immediate, involuntary movement of response.

"Do you want me, Megan?" he asked softly.

"Yes."

"Show me how much."

She wrapped her arms and legs about his body, clinging with a passionate abandon that left no room for inhibitions, no room for rational thought. His eyes blazed with a sudden flash of purely male triumph when he saw the extent of her arousal, and, his self-control finally at an end, he claimed her with a demanding urgency that drove her to the brink of ecstasy, then carried her over into the ultimate, shattering burst of pleasure and release.

Refuge In His Arms 137

* * *

When he finally eased himself away from her body, she was afraid to look at him. She realized instinctively that a watershed in her life had just been passed, but she was afraid to examine her emotions too closely for fear of what she might discover. She felt vulnerable from the top of her head down to the tips of her toes, and she knew that one scornful or demeaning remark would be enough to reduce her to tears. She wished she weren't so embarrassingly ignorant about the protocol of contemporary sexual relationships; she had no idea what to do next. On the rare occasions when Jeffrey had made love to her, they had been in bed with the blinds drawn and the lights out. Daylight passion, with her clothes scattered haphazardly along a riverbank, was entirely outside the scope of her experience.

She twisted her head away from him, trying to steel herself for the worst. Certainly her mother had complained often enough that men were brutes, only interested in a woman until they possessed her body.

Steve propped himself up on one elbow, and his bronzed fingers cupped her chin, pulling it determinedly around to face him. He brushed the wild tangle of her hair out of her eyes, and dropped a tender kiss on the end of her nose. "Megan, thank you," he said softly. "What we just shared—it was special for me."

The constriction around her heart seemed to loosen slightly. "It . . . it was pretty good for me, too," she managed to admit.

Some tiny sound or movement must have caught his attention. His head jerked up before she finished speaking, his body tensing instantaneously. Then the blue of his eyes warmed with the hint of laughter she always found so devastating. "I hate to tell you this, Meg," he said, "but we have an audience."

She whirled around, hands crossed over her breasts, and found herself staring straight into the dark eyes of a large, decidedly dirty sheep. The sheep stood very still, several strands of grass hanging from its mouth as it continued to chew contemplatively. After a few seconds of mutual, silent inspection, it turned tail and ambled off in the direction of the nearest hill.

Megan collapsed into laughter. "He looked very disapproving," she said.

"She. It was a female."

"How do you know?"

"I looked," he replied succinctly. "Besides, rams have horns."

He was still lying close to her, and his hands began to run lightly over her body. She was shocked when she felt herself begin to respond to his touch. Steve bent and kissed the soft underside of her breast. "I wish we could stay here," he said, "but I guess we'd better get dressed and make our way back to the cottage. Otherwise we just might meet up with the shepherd looking for his lost sheep."

Megan found her clothes and dressed quickly, feeling self-conscious as she raked her fingers through her mussed hair.

"I must look such a mess," she murmured.

He looked at her for a long time. "You look... loved," he said.

Chapter Nine

AFTER THEY HAD showered and changed, they cooked dinner together. Steve prepared shrimp creole, using freeze-dried shrimp and canned tomatoes. Megan, finding an unexpected supply of the best Swiss cooking chocolate, contributed a soufflé made with powdered milk and dried eggs. Despite the ingredients, she thought everything tasted delicious. In fact, she couldn't remember when she had last enjoyed a meal so much.

There was no wine or beer in the cottage—presumably government regulations forbade alcoholic merriment at the taxpayers' expense—but by the time they had cleared away the dishes and washed up, she felt as intoxicated as if she had consumed an entire bottle of champagne. Happiness, mingled with a throbbing undercurrent of sexual tension, bubbled irrepressibly in her veins.

Steve put the last dish away in the cupboard, then took her casually into his arms.

"You're sunburned," he said, running his finger gently across her cheekbones. "I'll check the first-aid supplies. There must be some lotion in there."

They found the large metal first-aid box in the bathroom cabinet and went into the bedroom to examine its contents. "Hold still," he said, rubbing the lotion lightly across her nose and under her eyes. He peered intently at her skin. "You'd better unbutton your shirt " he said. "Your throat and neck are beginning to turn red."

Megan kept her eyes lowered as she opened her blouse, strangely disoriented by the clinical detachment of his inspection and the nonchalance of his touch. A shadow of doubt touched her previous happiness. Steve's lovemaking that afternoon had been an entirely new experience for her, an earth-shattering revelation of her own sensuality. But perhaps for Steve it had been nothing much out of the ordinary. He was an extremely goodlooking and sexy man who exuded precisely the sort of devil-may-care aura of sensuality and danger that was calculated to appeal to women. He probably indulged in casual, friendly sex with half the attractive women he met, Megan thought gloomily. She mentally rubbed salt into her wounds. If the truth were known, he had probably found her a naive, stumbling lover and was simply too kind to tell her so.

She swallowed over the sudden lump in her throat, and Steve's fingers immediately halted their efficient ministrations. "What's the matter?" he asked. "Am I hurting you?"

"No! No, of course not."

"I'm all through, anyway." He leaned across her to put the bottle of lotion down on the bedside table, and his arm brushed her breasts. She blushed hotly when she felt her nipples tauten in a humiliatingly visible response to his touch.

He straightened from his task, and she saw a twinkle of wicked amusement gleaming in his eyes. His hands trailed with tantalizing suggestiveness inside the lace edge of her bra. "Well, now, this is beginning to look like a highly promising situation," he murmured. "Do you have any special plans for the rest of the evening, Ms. Richards?"

She licked her dry lips, taking her courage in both hands. "Yes," she said.

He was clearly surprised by her answer. "You do? What are they?"

"This," she breathed. She stepped into the circle of his arms and reached up to kiss his mouth with a fierce intensity that astonished them both.

His arms tightened around her, and he gave back kiss for kiss. "Megan," he muttered as his mouth trailed a line of torrid kisses over her neck and along her shoulders. "Oh, God, Megan, I only have to look at you and I want you."

"Then look at me," she whispered, wondering fleetingly what had happened to twenty-seven years of inhibitions. "Look at all of me," she said huskily. She shrugged out of her blouse, letting it fall unheeded to the floor. Then her hands moved to the zipper of her jeans and pushed slowly downward.

Steve didn't say anything, but his eyes darkened and a slow wave of color washed into his cheeks as she stepped out of her jeans and tossed them into a corner of the bedroom. When she unclipped her bra, he made a quick, strangled exclamation and pulled her roughly into his arms, thrusting his hands into her hair and tipping her head back to receive his kiss.

They were both on fire with passion. When he finally carried her to the bed, she was wild with wanting him, and his breath came in low uneven gasps. They twisted together in the cool sheets, hands and mouths seeking hungrily. When they reached the ultimate pinnacle of excitement, they hovered there, filled with an exquisite moment of mutual longing, until they exploded together in the tumultuous descent into ecstasy.

They awoke the next morning to another day of brilliant sunshine. The sky was a cloudless arc of clear blue, and there wasn't a trace of humidity in the air. The mist and rain, for which Wales was notorious, were conspicuously absent.

They spent the day outdoors, wandering along the banks of the river, finding endless topics of conversation to fill the long, sun-filled hours. Steve spoke about his family, and Megan drank in the information, not asking herself why she found his life history so fascinating. His father was a building contractor, his mother a high school chemistry teacher. He had one younger sister who was married, the mother of twin sons and part owner of a furniture store. Before her marriage, Steve said, his sister had worked as an interior decorator. He had trained as a chemical engineer and worked briefly as a research scientist before joining the CIA.

In return, Megan confided something about her own youth, glossing over the difficulties of growing up in a household filled with constantly changing stepfathers and siblings, and concentrating instead on the friends she had made at school and the satisfaction she derived from her career.

In the late afternoon they pulled two chairs out of the living room and sat in the garden, sipping lemonade.

"The honeysuckle smells wonderful, doesn't it?" Steve said.

"Mmmm." Megan leaned back in her chair, closing her eyes and feeling the early evening sun dance on her eyelids. She felt lazy and blissfully indolent. "Have you ever been married, Steve?" she asked suddenly, not quite sure where the question sprang from.

"No. In my job, marriage is almost impossible."

"Why's that? I thought the government was all in favor of family life."

"Maybe, but not for its undercover agents. Field assignments are given only to single people, usually men. You can't have an operative worrying all the time about what will happen to his wife and family. Those worries interfere with efficiency. There's no room for emotional entanglements in my line of work."

A faint chill struck her at the ruthlessness of his statement. "But you aren't going to work on undercover assignments anymore," she murmured. "You're going back to Washington."

For the first time since they arrived at the cottage, she became aware of a certain strain in Steve's manner. "I haven't accepted that assignment yet," he said tersely. "I want to work in the field. It's what I've been trained for; it's what I'm good at." He got up from the chair and leaned against the high stone wall, toying abstractedly with a strand of honeysuckle. "I'm fighting my assignment back to Washington every step of the way. Just because my cover was blown in Luxembourg doesn't mean that I can't be reassigned somewhere else. Marriage isn't in my plans for the future, Megan. It probably never will be."

She felt a stab of fierce pain somewhere in the region of her midriff, but she was too proud to let him see how his words had affected her. Besides, she reminded herself, Steve's marital plans were no concern of hers. After her experience with Jeffrey, the last thing in the world she wanted was to get entangled in a serious relationship with a man like Steve. She felt nothing for him except an intense physical attraction, and that was no foundation for a long-term relationship. It was no foundation for anything worthwhile; she knew that from her parents' endless series of unsatisfactory marriages.

"I can understand your feelings," she said, managing to speak with convincing lightness. "Secret agents and marriage don't seem to mix well together." She stood up, stretching elaborately and pretending to yawn. "Shall I go and see what I can find for us to eat? I think I might go to bed early tonight."

"Sounds like a good idea," he said. "I have to make a routine call to headquarters within the next hour. I'll do it while you're fixing dinner."

She heated canned breasts of chicken with mushrooms and peas, and spread garlic butter on some dinner rolls she found in the freezer. The supply cupboard was well stocked with canned fruit, so for dessert she chilled some raspberries.

When the meal was ready, she stuck her head into the living room to call Steve. She found him standing by one of the windows, staring out into the garden, and the expression on his face was so grim that for a moment she was frightened.

"Steve," she said hesitantly, "dinner's ready."

He swung round to face her, and she saw that the bleakness of his expression had already been replaced by his old mask of cool indifference.

"Um... have you made your call to headquarters?" she asked.

"Oh, yes, I made my call." He pushed his hand through his hair in an abrupt, careless gesture. "I'll be right with you," he said.

"Steve, what is it? What's happened?"

There was a moment of tense silence. "Dr. Helen Meaney has disappeared—in case you didn't know."

"But that's wonderful!" she exclaimed, feeling a wave of relief wash over her. Now the authorities would surely believe that she hadn't been helping Jeffrey. Helen Meaney's disappearance virtually proved that Jeffrey's assistant had also been his accomplice.

The implication of Steve's words pierced her euphoria. "What do you mean, *in case I didn't know?* How could I possibly know what Dr. Meaney has done? I've been here with you for the past two days."

His eyes were impenetrable pools of indigo, hiding his thoughts completely, and when he spoke, his voice was devoid of expression. "While we were driving to London to have lunch with your friend Sally, I told you that Jeffrey Brookfield's papers were forged. I told you that we had found no record of Helen Meaney's birth or early education. I told you that Inspector Browning was about to pay a call on Dr. Meaney and ask her some very important questions. In fact, I gave you a lot of vital, confidential information. As soon as you got a chance, you made an excuse to slip away from me. When I found you again, you were with two KGB men. I have no idea what they said to you or you said to them, but twelve hours later Helen Meaney disappeared, taking a great deal of research data with her."

Megan was sure that every trace of color drained out of her cheeks. "What are you trying to accuse me of, Steve?"

"Nothing—yet."

"But later? When you've had a chance to find some more so-called proof?"

"I don't know." He turned away and took up his previous position by the window. "Everything I told you during the drive to London I had been instructed by my superiors to pass on," he said tonelessly. "They wanted to see what you would do with the information I gave you."

"I didn't do anything with it," she said fiercely.

"Didn't you? In view of what's happened, I think it's logical to conclude you warned those two KBG agents that Helen Meaney was under suspicion and about to be questioned by Scotland Yard. In other words, you passed on secret information just as fast as you could."

All the threads of what he was saying finally came together in her mind. "The information you gave me about Jeffrey..." she whispered. "My God, Steve, you weren't trying to make me feel better about his defection. You were deliberately trying to set me up!"

He continued to stare out of the window. "No," he said. "I was trying to prove your innocence."

"You don't seem to have done a very good job," she exclaimed, choking back a bitter laugh. "When you were

Refuge In His Arms 147

making all those great arrangements to set me up, didn't you have the sense to put a tail on Helen Meaney?"

"Damn it, of course there was a tail on Dr. Meaney! The department used three of its best people. Helen Meaney managed to shake them all while she was at the lab."

"She sounds like an experienced conspirator," Megan said.

"We think so." After a brief pause, he added, "The security agencies are working on the assumption that neither Helen Meaney nor Jeffrey Brookfield was actually a British citizen. We think they were probably Russian-born scientists, trained to infiltrate a key Western research project. We think they were both five or six years older than they claimed, already fully-qualified when they entered British universities."

"Why are you telling me all this, Steve? Are you waiting to see if I pass this exciting new information on to somebody lurking out there on the hillside—one of the sheep, maybe?"

"I told you because I thought you might want to know the truth about Jeffrey Brookfield. He wasn't a treacherous Englishman; he was a dedicated Russian spy."

Megan looked at the hard, tense line of Steve's shoulders and, for no reason she could understand, all traces of anger drained out of her. A shiver of bittersweet awareness rippled down her spine.

"Steve," she said softly, "you can't possibly believe that I warned Helen Meaney to run away. Why would I do something so crazy? I *wanted* her to answer all your questions! Don't you see, if she admits she's Jeffrey's collaborator, there's no reason to suspect me!"

He turned to look at her, but there was no hint of softening in his rigid stance. "Unfortunately, there's no reason why Jeffrey Brookfield couldn't have had more than one person helping him. Dr. Meaney's actions made no difference to the facts of your own situation."

Her fingers knotted into a tight ball of frustration. "The fact is, you don't want to believe I'm innocent, do you, Steve?"

He gave a harsh laugh. "You can think that if you like."

She detected a further tightening of the grim lines around his mouth, and she shrugged, aware of a deep sensation of loss. "Well, I guess there's nothing more to be said. I can only hope the security forces catch up with Helen Meaney soon."

She walked hurriedly toward the stairs, not prepared to let him see the tears already hovering on the ends of her lashes. She had to fight against an irrational feeling of desolation. There was no reason to allow Steve Callahan's lack of trust to upset her. His good opinion wasn't important. In a few days he would have gone out of her life, as swiftly as he had entered it.

She swallowed hard, trying desperately to keep her voice low and even when she spoke again. "Dinner is in the oven, if you want to help yourself. I don't think I'll join you. I'm not very hungry at the moment."

She was less than halfway up the stairs when he caught up with her, clutching her arm and forcing her to turn around and face him. He stared down at her for a long time, his eyes dark and brooding, then he reached up and touched her wet lashes.

The gentleness of his touch was her undoing. The tears she had been fighting to hide welled up and poured silently down her cheeks. His arms tightened around her. Then he gave a shuddering sigh as he bent his head to kiss her tear-stained cheeks. When she tried to twist away from him, he grabbed a handful of her long, dark hair and pulled her head up so that her mouth was exposed to his. He kissed her with a brutal, consuming passion that subdued her defiance and left her melting against his body. His hands slid from her hair to scoop her up into his arms. He carried her up the few remaining stairs, kicked the bedroom door open, and put her down on one of the twin beds.

Neither of them spoke. He lay on top of her, pinning her to the bed. His expression was harsh, but his eyes burned with a dark, hot flame as he ripped off her clothes and tore impatiently at his own shirt and jeans, indifferent to buttons and fastenings. Megan knew she ought to resist him, but the truth was that his urgency excited her, and she wanted him every bit as much as he wanted her.

He kissed her repeatedly, on her eyes, her face, her breasts, and she met the desperate hunger of his touch with an answering hunger of her own. She clung to him, feeling the raw need that surged through him, and eager to meet it.

Steve hadn't spoken a single word since he caught up with her on the stairs, and her thoughts suddenly seemed to echo endlessly in the silence of the darkened room. *She loved him*. She loved Steve Callahan. That was why the days in his company passed so quickly. That was why he could make her tremble with a single, brief glance. That was why she was so hurt by his suspicions. That was why she wanted him to make love to her with such painful, feverish intensity.

The realization of her love spun in her head as he caressed her, alternately terrifying her and warming her with its sweetness. She longed to murmur the truth of her feelings against Steve's heated flesh, but some remaining trace of common sense kept her silent. In the end, when she parted her thighs to receive him, she had to bite her lips to keep from crying out the words of love he didn't want to hear. His passion swiftly carried her with him to the ultimate physical heights, and while her body clung to him in helpless surrender, her heart guarded the secret of the love she knew he didn't want.

When it was all over, he went into the bathroom and put on his robe. He paused in the doorway to tie the belt. "Do you want to eat dinner now?" he asked. They were the first words he had spoken since they left the living room.

"No, thank you. I'm not hungry."

He came and stood by the side of the bed, not touching her. "Megan...I was rough. Did I...hurt you?"

Yes! she wanted to cry out. Yes, you hurt me. You've destroyed defenses it took me twenty-seven years to build, and I'm aching with the pain of it. She closed her eyes and turned her head away from him. "No," she said flatly, "you didn't hurt me at all."

It was late when he came to bed, but Megan wasn't asleep. She lay curled down under the bedcovers, taking care to keep her face in shadow so that Steve wouldn't be able to see that she was awake. He made almost no noise at all as he slipped off his robe and got quietly into the other bed. She listened intently, guessing that it was less than ten minutes before his breathing slowed and he fell asleep.

She sighed and turned on her back to stare up at the sliver of moonlight dancing on the ceiling. What had she wanted him to do? More to the point, what had she expected him to do, other than go to sleep? Steve had never tried to deceive her about his feelings or his intentions. He had told her he wanted her, that he found her body beautiful. He had never suggested that he loved her, or even hinted that he liked her company. At the first possible opportunity, he had warned her that he didn't plan to marry.

Megan stirred restlessly on the bed. The mattress, which earlier had comfortably held both her and Steve, now seemed too narrow for comfort. The sheets seemed scratchy against her skin, although last night they had seemed cool and inviting.

A breeze lifted the edge of the curtain, briefly revealing the clear night sky and the full moon. Megan thought suddenly how refreshing it would be to take a walk in the garden, breathing in the nighttime scents of wild flowers and tall grasses. She glanced toward Steve and saw that he still slept, so she slid out of bed as quietly as she could, not wanting to disturb him. She picked up her sneakers and her jeans and shirt as she crept out of the bedroom and down the stairs. She stopped by the front door to get dressed, then quietly pulled back the bolts and slipped out into the garden.

The sky was a cloudless black dome overhead, pierced by hundreds of pinpoints of starlight and the silver glow of the moon. Megan walked along the gravel path that circled the house, relieved to feel some of her tension unwinding as the peacefulness of the night enveloped her. When she reached the high wall surrounding the house, she searched for a small section that was free of flowers and leaned against the cool stones, staring out into the velvet darkness. She spotted a particularly beautiful wild rose growing on a thorny branch a few inches out of her reach. It glowed with an exotic creamy pallor in the moonlight, and she stretched across the wall, trying to pick it. She was leaning halfway across the stones when she felt herself seized roughly from behind, steel arms clamping around her waist.

She recognized Steve's touch instantly, but a scream tore from her lips in an automatic, reflex reaction. He clamped his hand over her mouth with bruising force and swept her up into his arms.

"Don't say *anything!*" he ordered in a low voice that throbbed with repressed fury.

She struggled to free herself as he strode back toward the cottage, but it was like fighting against the bonds of a straitjacket. She bit his hand, furious at his unreasonable treatment of her, but he totally ignored her attacks even though she knew she must have hurt him. She could feel the butt of his gun pressing against her breasts, and she shivered at the knowledge that he had taken the time to strap on his shoulder holster before coming in search of her. What had he expected to find?

Once they were inside the cottage, he carried her upstairs and dumped her roughly on the bed. "Stay there. Don't move and don't speak," he said curtly.

She rubbed her fingers over her sore mouth. "What have I done?" she said furiously. "Why are you acting like this? I went for a walk; that's all!"

"At two in the morning? Having taken great pains not to wake me? Just who are you hoping to fool, Megan?"

"Not you," she said bitterly. "You can do that all by yourself."

"By myself—with a little bit of help from you. You're dynamite in bed, Megan, I'll grant you that, but I'm not quite so besotted with you as to believe everything you whisper in my ear when we're making love. I still have some powers of judgment left."

"Obviously not enough," she said through gritted teeth. "I couldn't sleep, and I went out into the garden for a while. What's so mysterious about that?"

"There's nothing mysterious about it at all. You were specifically told never to go out alone." He strode over to the door. "I'm calling the local security services to have them run a quick sweep of the locality. Let's hope for your sake that there are no KGB agents out there."

"Don't be ridiculous, Steve," she said wearily.

He didn't answer her. He walked out of the bedroom, turning the key in the lock with a sharp, authoritative click.

She was sitting on the bed, knees pulled up to her chin, when he unlocked the bedroom door over an hour later. She stared straight ahead, refusing to ask him for any information.

He stood at the end of the bed, his mouth compressing into a grim, taut line as he looked at her. "Don't you want to know whether we found your friends?" he asked mockingly.

"I have no friends in this area."

"So you don't know anything about the little campsite the security officers found a mile downstream from here?"

She looked up quickly, her eyes widening with shock. "You found... they found some people *watching* us?"

He walked over to the other bed, a grimace of disgust shadowing his tanned features. "You don't have to worry, Megan," he said wearily. "Your scream warned them in time. They got away. We only found the traces of their equipment."

She sprang off the bed, grasping both his arms in her impatience to convince him of her innocence. "Steve, don't be like this! You don't really think I was trying to contact those men!" Her voice softened into a husky plea. "Steve, it's crazy for you to be angry with me. You know how much... how much we've shared. Please trust me."

There was a long moment of silence in the room. Then he turned away from her, pulling the covers of his bed up from the floor where they had fallen.

"I'm a federal agent on active duty," he said neutrally. "It's my responsibility to keep you safe in this cottage. My personal... feelings for you have nothing to do with anything." He unzipped his cotton jacket and dropped it onto a chair as he got into bed. He didn't take off his jeans or unbuckle his holster.

"Perhaps you'd better get some sleep," he said, clasping his hands beneath his head and staring up at the ceiling. "It's almost dawn."

Megan turned slowly away from him. She went back to her bed and punched angrily at the pillow. She crawled under the sheet, pulling it almost up to her ears. The silence in the little bedroom was oppressive, but neither of them broke it.

She stared dry-eyed into the darkness until the sun came up and the birds started their dawn chorus. She lay wide awake, hating herself, because she knew in her innermost heart that, despite everything Steve had said and done, if he crossed the two feet of space separating their beds and took her into his arms, she would welcome him with a passion inflamed, not sated, by the lovemaking they had already shared.

Chapter Ten

THE NIGHT HADN'T brought much sleep, but Megan was relieved to find that it had given her a small measure of wisdom. She had allowed her feelings for Steve to run out of control, she decided, simply because he had entered her life at a point when Jeffrey's defection had left her acutely vulnerable. She had never loved Jeffrey, but for a brief time she had counted on building a stable future with him. In the beginning she had even looked forward to the prospect of having children to love and cherish as she had never been loved by her own parents. Jeffrey had temporarily destroyed all her dreams of a relationship built on the solid ground of friendship and common interests, but that didn't mean such dreams were gone forever. Another man would come along, who was sensible and undemanding—a gentle, unassuming man who didn't threaten her sense of self in the way Steve Callahan did.

Megan was quite pleased with her newly recovered common sense. By the time she had taken a shower, she had convinced herself that she would never have been so foolishly drawn to Steve if the circumstances of their meeting hadn't been so extraordinary.

When she went down to breakfast, she felt more in command of her wayward emotions than she had for several days. She sat across the breakfast table from Steve and deliberately hardened her heart to his attractions. There could never be any future for her in a relationship with him, and it was time she protected her battered feelings by bringing their time together to an immediate end. It was being so close to him, she reasoned, that was causing all the trouble. Once she was away from him, she would quickly forget him. After all, there was nothing binding them together except a high-voltage charge of raw physical attraction.

As she finished her breakfast, her eyes accidentally met Steve's, and she felt the inevitable, unwelcome crumbling of her defenses. She quickly rebuilt them, willing herself not to respond to the tenderness she saw in her gaze. She was probably confusing the shadows left by fatigue with the softness caused by genuine emotion. She gathered up the plates and the empty coffee cups and walked briskly to the sink, turning on the hot water as she spoke.

"I've been doing some thinking," she said, swishing the dishes around in the soapy water. "And I've reached some important decisions. I'm tired of being manipulated by other people, Steve, and I intend to put a stop to it."

"I don't think you've been manipulated—"

"I'm tired of being suspected," Megan interrupted him. "I want to speak to my lawyer, which is something I should have done days ago. I haven't been trying to contact any Soviet agents, I haven't the slightest intention of defecting to any Communist bloc country, and you have no right to keep me in confinement. I want to go back to Cambridge *today*—right now—so that I can start making preparation to leave that cottage. It was Jeffrey's, not mine, and I don't want to stay there now that I know the truth about him."

Steve stood up. "We've discussed all this before, Megan. You can call your lawyer if you wish, but it won't make any difference. He'll advise you to cooperate with us. He'll simply point out to you all the advantages of remaining in our protective custody."

"My lawyer is a woman," she said. "And I don't think you should presume to speak for her. I doubt if her opinion of your so-called protective custody would be very flattering."

Steve picked up a cloth and began drying the breakfast dishes she had already washed. "I know I've handled things... unprofessionally," he said, his voice sounding strained. "You would be within your rights to request a different agent to protect you, Megan. Maybe that would make the situation here more acceptable to you."

"What reason would I give for requesting a different guard?" she asked. "Shall I tell them we're incompatible, or that I prefer secret service agents with dark hair?"

He turned away, ignoring her sarcasm, and for a few moments seemed totally occupied with stacking crockery in one of the cupboards. "You could tell the truth," he said finally. "You have grounds for entering a complaint of sexual harassment."

Megan was momentarily stunned. She found it intolerable to think that Steve might view the beauty of their lovemaking as nothing more than a sordid episode of profesional misconduct. He had said that he found their lovemaking special and, even though he had never pretended to have any deep emotional commitment to her, she hadn't thought he would lie. She glanced toward him and saw the pallor underneath the bronze gleam of his tan. The suggestion he had just made, she realized suddenly, had not been an easy one. He was laying his career on the line, and it was just possible, she thought, that she had misinterpreted the reasons behind his suggestion.

"I would never do that, Steve," she said softly. "I don't want to ruin your career."

"The charges would be justified," he replied, his voice unnaturally stiff.

She was infuriated by his sense of honor. She wanted him to love her, passionately and irrevocably, not to feel a sense of obligation toward her. "Don't be such a damned, old-fashioned chauvinist, Steve," she said heatedly. "There was no sexual harassment. I was a willing partner, not a helpless victim."

He studied her intently for several seconds in a way that made her pulse race, but he didn't reply, and eventually her gaze dropped to her hands. She saw that they were shaking, and she thrust them into the pockets of her jeans before walking away from the sink and sitting at the kitchen table.

"A different guard would make no difference at all," she said, as soon as she was sure she had her voice reasonably under control. "I've told you I want to talk to my lawyer. I don't think this case has been investigated properly so far. I don't think the CIA and Special Branch have asked the right questions. I've told you a dozen times that I don't want to contact the KGB and that I don't want to join Jeffrey in Moscow. What does it mean to your investigation if I'm telling the truth? If the KGB men don't really expect to make contact with me, why are they allowing themselves to be so visible?"

He shrugged. "You tell me. You seem to have a theory."

"I think it's because they want to draw attention toward me and away from somebody else. In my opinion, you wasted your time when you instructed the British security forces to search along the riverbanks outside this cottage last night. The men would have been better employed searching the coast for Helen Meaney."

"Virtually every law-enforcement officer in Britain is already looking for Dr. Meaney," Steve said curtly. "Every port and airport has extra guards on duty. We've issued descriptions of her through the media to the general public. Air traffic controllers have been warned to keep watch for unauthorized aircraft. Believe me, nobody is taking Helen Meaney's disappearance lightly, least of all me."

"That's great news," she said, unable to avoid a touch of irony from entering her voice. "Let's just hope you're more successful in keeping track of her movements than you were in keeping track of Jeffrey's. But in the meantime, while we're waiting for her to be found, I'd like to call my lawyer. And I mean right now, Steve."

"You have the legal right to counsel if you insist on it," he said coolly. "Come into the living room. The only phone in this cottage connects directly with Scotland Yard. It's a scrambled line to prevent wiretapping. But I'll have the Special Branch operator connect you to a regular outside line, and you can place the call to your lawyer yourself."

She waited impatiently while he went through the seemingly endless ritual of punching codes into the special phone and then identifying himself to a succession of listeners. Eventually Megan realized he was talking to Inspector Sidney Browning.

As always, Steve's side of the conversation revealed little but, after five minutes or so, he hung up the phone without passing it over to Megan. When she started to protest, he cut in abruptly.

"It's all over, Megan. There's no need to call your lawyer. Dr. Helen Meaney was picked up at Prestwick Airport in Scotland at dawn this morning. She was using forged papers in an effort board a flight leaving for Norway. She isn't saying much, but from the little she has said, and from the checks he's now completed on your background, Inspector Browning considers it quite safe for you to return to Cambridge."

"I see. My need for *protection* is suddenly over."

Steve refused to rise to her provocation. "Yes," he said. "Inspector Browning thinks all danger of kidnapping is past. A police guard will be on duty outside your house in Cambridge for another twenty-four hours. By then, all press interest in you should be at an end. If it's not, you can make a request for continued protection by a uniformed police officer." He spoke dryly, as if he were quoting from a handbook of police rules.

"What will happen...?" Megan swallowed over the burning constriction in her throat and tried again. "What will you do next, Steve? I mean you personally."

"I have to wait for new orders," he said. "I suppose I'll be flying back to Washington soon."

As if on cue, they heard the crunch of tires on the gravel driveway, and through the window Megan saw a police squad car stop and park in the shade of an apple tree. A policeman in uniform, with the three stripes of a sergeant on his sleeves, got out of the car and walked to the door. A moment later the doorbell buzzed.

Steve went to answer it, gesturing to indicate that Megan should stay in the center of the living room. He unbolted the door cautiously, leaving the chain in place until the policeman displayed his official identification. Steve handed back the identity card, unfastened the chain, and opened the door.

"Come in, Sergeant," he said.

The police officer entered the living room, nodding cordially toward Steve. "Good morning. You must be Agent Callahan, and how are you? I'm Sergeant Davies, as you saw on my I.D."

"Yes, I'm Callahan. And this is Megan Brookfield."

"Good morning, Mrs. Brookfield. You have a lovely name, to be sure. Did you know a long time ago one of our Welsh princesses was called Megan?"

She smiled, warming to his friendliness. "I knew it was a Welsh name, although I can't claim any ancestors from this part of the world, I'm afraid."

"Well, it seems our old names are getting popular on the other side of the Atlantic. And how have you enjoyed your stay here, Mrs. Brookfield?"

She couldn't look at Steve. "It's been very nice, thank you."

"Yes, we've been having a lovely little bit of sunshine

this week. Makes up for our terrible spring. In this part of Wales it never stopped raining for three weeks together during April." The sergeant shook his head in mournful memory. He was a ruddy-cheeked older man who spoke with the distinctive, lilting accent of the Welsh countryside. He seemed all set for a lengthy chat, when Steve intervened.

"Do you have a message for us, Sergeant Davies?"

"There now! I was forgetting you didn't know why I've come." The sergeant carefully unbuttoned his navy blue jacket and withdrew a sealed envelope from his inner pocket. "I'm to have the pleasure of driving the young lady back to Cambridge," he said. "And I understand this letter I have for you contains your orders, sir. There's a military plane leaving for Andrews Air Force Base this afternoon, and I believe some important people in Washington are expecting you to catch it."

Steve glanced at his watch, them ripped open the slim package the sergeant had handed him and swiftly read the two papers it contained. He looked once toward Megan when he had finished reading, then slipped the papers back into the envelope and turned to face the sergeant.

"If you and Mrs. Brookfield would be good enough to make sure that the kitchen is clean, with all the provisions stored in airtight containers, I'll pack our belongings and straighten up the bedroom. You have to leave before I do, because it's my responsibility to see that the cottage is left secure until the official cleaners are sent in."

"Very good, sir."

She turned uncertainly toward Steve. "I ought to pack my own suitcase," she said.

"I can take care of that for you, Mrs. Brookfield."

Refuge In His Arms 163

She paled at the coolness of his words. "I wouldn't want to put you to any trouble."

"It's no trouble, Mrs. Brookfield. But we are working under a certain amount of time pressure if I'm going to catch that plane."

"Of course. Don't let me hold you up, Agent Callahan." She swung away abruptly and hurried across the room toward the kitchen. The sergeant followed close behind.

Despite his slow speech and portly build, the sergeant was a quick and efficient worker. With his help, it was only a matter of minutes until the perishable foodstuffs were sealed into plastic containers and the garbage disposed of inside a thick paper bag lined with foil.

"We'll put this outside the gate, and it will be collected by the dustmen tomorrow," the sergeant said, picking up the bag. He looked around the immaculate kitchen with a beam of approval. "Nice place, this. I've never been inside here before. The kitchen has all the latest conveniences, doesn't it?"

"Yes, it's a very comfortable cottage," Megan said, surprised to discover that her voice sounded almost normal. She wondered how she could sound like a rational, functioning human being when inside she was collapsing into a heap of emotional rubble. She smiled brightly. "Since we're all through here, I think maybe I'll see if I can help Mr. Callahan with anything."

"There's no need." Steve appeared at the kitchen doorway. His own canvas traveling bag was slung over one shoulder, and he carried Megan's small suitcase in his hand. "Everything's cleared away upstairs," he said to the sergeant. "If you and Mrs. Brookfield would like to leave now, I'll run one final check on the window bolts before I lock up the front entrance."

"Very good, sir." There was no doubt that Steve Callahan's official rank, whatever it was, was sufficiently high to impress the police sergeant. His manner was deferential in the extreme.

"We'll be on our way, shall we?" Sergeant Davies smiled at Megan. "I expect you'll be pleased to get back to your own home."

"Very pleased." She gave a tiny gasp of laughter and heard the hysteria pushing far too close to the surface. "There's no place like home," she said, the words almost choking her. Involuntarily she looked at Steve. His brilliant blue eyes were partly concealed behind hooded lids, so that she couldn't read his expression, but his mouth was curved into a polite smile that embraced her and the police sergeant with equal lack of emotion. He nodded to the sergeant, then held out his hand to her with the same impersonal courtesy he might have extended to a total stranger.

"Good-bye, Mrs. Brookfield. I hope you have a good journey back to Cambridge." His voice was as devoid of emotion as his smile, and to her overwrought senses he sounded supremely indifferent to her imminent departure.

She took his hand, and the pain of the meaningless contact was so intense that the hurt exploded inside her, leaving a residue of anguish so fierce that she scarcely knew how to contain it.

"Good-bye, Agent Callahan." She heard the catch in her voice, barely concealed behind the cold formality of her words, and she walked quickly toward the front door, afraid that the tears choking the back of her throat would spill out and betray her.

"Megan..."

His voice stopped her on the threshold. She turned in his direction, but she didn't see him because her eyes were blinded by unshed tears. "Yes?"

"Just good-bye, I guess. And... take care."

She twisted around, fumbling with the front door handle. At last the door was open, and she ran across the courtyard to the squad car. It was unlocked, and she slid onto the hot vinyl seat, shuddering with the relief of being away from him before she broke down and made an utter fool of herself. In less than a minute the sergeant had joined her in the car. When they drove out of the cottage grounds onto the narrow, rutted roadway, Steve still hadn't appeared at the front door.

Sergeant Davies kept up a stream of easygoing chatter all the way back to Cambridge, apparently untroubled by the fact that Megan's answers were rarely more than monosyllables and sometimes incoherent monosyllables at that.

The sun was still shining with an unrelenting, un-English heat when they arrived at her house. The stones of the cottage gleamed with a stark gray brilliance in the harshness of the early afternoon light, and, as Megan got out of the car, she was swept by an immense reluctance to enter the house and pick up the tangled threads of her old life. Almost before she was aware of what she was planning, she turned to speak to the sergeant.

"I don't think I can... I don't want to go in," she said. "Would you mind driving me to a hotel? There's quite a pleasant inn just around the corner from here."

Sergeant Davies surveyed her with a great deal of sympathy and an unwelcome degree of understanding.

"It will be my pleasure, Mrs. Brookfield," he said neutrally, adding nothing more that was remotely personal until she had signed in at the reception desk of the hotel and been given the keys to a room on the second floor.

His brown eyes were shrewd as he shook her hand outside the cream-painted door of her bedroom. "I daresay Agent Callahan will be in touch shortly," he said. "I was told they want him back in the States urgently. He's their expert on nuclear technology, you know."

"Thank you very much for escorting me back to Cambridge, Sergeant Davies. I really appreciate your kindness during the journey, but Agent Callahan's movements are no concern of mine." She was quite pleased with the polite note of indifference she managed to inject into her words. She had never known until these past few days what a gifted actress she actually was.

"Is that so?" The sergeant smiled slightly, and his ruddy cheeks crumpled into well-worn laughter creases. "Well, I've been with the police for nearly thirty years, Mrs. Brookfield, and I'm not so sure. You don't spend thirty years on the force without learning to spot somebody who's not telling the whole truth about a situation." He gave her no opportunity to say anything further because he was speaking again almost before she'd assimilated the significance of his words.

"Have a good rest, Mrs. Brookfield. I enjoyed the drive myself, and I wish you every success in the future. Remember, just for the next day or so be extra cautious. Don't open the door to anybody until you know for sure who it is. Oh, I nearly forgot to mention: Inspector Browning will be contacting you before the end of the week."

He touched his uniform hat in a brief salute, then

disappeared quickly down the stairs. Megan went into her room and tossed her suitcase onto a chair at the same time as she kicked off her shoes, leaving them lying haphazardly on the bedside rug. Feeling uncomfortably hot and sticky, she stripped off her shirt and let it fall in a heap on the bed. The hotel room already looked more untidy than the house had ever looked during the whole time she'd been living there with Jeffrey. She shrugged, indifferent to the mess, and threw herself down on the bed, staring unseeingly at the Victorian moldings on the high ceiling.

Her practical problems were virtually over, she realized, and Inspector Browning would no doubt clear up any lingering loose ends when he next got in touch with her. Now all she had to do was concentrate on curing the minor emotional problem of a broken heart.

That ought to be easy enough to accomplish, she thought. Steve Callahan was out of her life, finally and irrevocably. It was what she wanted, of course. Emotional entanglements weren't for her. She was sensible and clear-headed and dedicated to her career. In a week—maybe less—she would certainly have forgotten Steve.

A sharp pain shot through her, and she rolled over onto her stomach, burying her face the lumpy hotel pillow. I *will* forget him, she vowed silently, clenching her hands into two tight, determined fists. He means nothing to me. She pulled one of the pillows over her head and tried hard to ignore the restless ache in her heart, an ache that ought to have warned her how much she lied.

Chapter Eleven

MEGAN FOLDED THE small blanket and pushed it down into a corner of the heavy-duty cardboard packing case. All the upstairs closets of the cottage were now completely empty, and she breathed a weary sigh of relief as she sealed the final carton with gray strapping tape. Two efficient packers from the moving company had left half an hour earlier, having carefully wrapped and crated the few breakable items that belonged to her, rather than to Jeffrey. Tomorrow she would take the cartons to the airport and send them back to Washington by air freight. Sally had agreed to store Megan's belongings until she found a new job and somewhere to live.

She stretched, her muscles feeling cramped after too many hours of bending and stooping. Several wayward strands of hair fell forward over her eyes, and she pushed at them impatiently, trying to poke them back into her pony tail. After a couple of unsuccessful attempts she gave up and pulled off the elastic band, combing her long hair free with her fingers.

She hadn't bothered to eat any lunch, and it was already late afternoon. She didn't have much appetite— she never did these days—but she went down to the kitchen to make herself a cup of coffee. She put the kettle on to boil, then glanced absentmindedly out of the window, watching the rain fall in a steady, unrelenting sheet that bounced hard off the outside windowsills. The unseasonably warm weather had ended before the middle of June and, for the last two weeks, it seemed to Megan that the rain had been never-ending. A suitable accompaniment to her gloomy mood, she thought wryly, as she spooned instant coffee into a mug.

The kettle boiled, and she made herself a cup of black instant coffee. She sat at the kitchen table to drink it, reaching for Sally's letter, which she had been too busy to open when it arrived in the morning mail. She smiled as she read her friend's breezy acocunt of the dramas of summer life in a big city hospital. July was always a busy month in the maternity wards: a direct consequence, Sally pointed out irreverently, of the long cold nights of October and November. Megan could almost hear her friend's voice laughing up at her from the pages, and her smile didn't fade until she got to the final few paragraphs.

"I've saved the best news till last," Sally had written. "You'll probably be astonished to hear that I'm madly in love. I can't believe I'm nearly twenty-seven years old and never knew the difference between sexual attraction and love before. Why didn't anybody tell me that love could make you feel so weird, so completely disoriented? I met Greg—he's a pediatrician—after I got back from the London conference last month and immediately decided to marry him. He doesn't know it yet, but his bachelor days are definitely numbered. He's still wriggling around a bit, trying to fight the inevitable (he sees himself as Heaven's personal gift to the women of the world), but I figure that by the end of August he'll have given up and accepted his fate. He already looks worried every time I come into the room—it reminds me of the way Steve Callahan looked at you that day we had lunch together in London—with a mixture of longing and grim resistance.

"I never told you how much I liked Steve. He's a great guy, Megan, and I think you should grab him. I'd be after him myself if Greg didn't curl my toes every time I look at him. Do you know I mean that literally? My toe muscles have an automatic, reflexive reaction every time Greg walks into the room. It's the most extraordinary sensation. What he does to my pulse rate, of course, is indescribable... even for a nurse!"

Megan let the letter fall out of her hand onto the table. She stared blindly at the yellow kitchen wall, wondering why it had taken her so long to acknowledge the truth about her feelings for Steve. Why couldn't she ever be honest about her own emotions, just as Sally was? She had originally learned to hide her feelings from her parents as a desperate method of emotional self-defense, but she was an adult now, and it was time she grew out of such immature protective devices. There was no need for her to spend the rest of her life afraid of her own feelings. Love, if she gave it freely, couldn't possibly hurt as much as living a life squeezed dry of all warmth and affection.

Megan forced herself to face up to the true facts of her situation. She was leaving England and returning to Washington because she wanted to find Steve Callahan, and not for any of the other reasons she had managed to dream up. Why couldn't she be honest with herself and admit how important Steve was to her happiness? Without him, her world was gray and flat and achingly empty.

She had found it amazingly easy to forget her brief, unsatisfactory relationship with Jeffrey, but it had been impossible to forget Steve. Memories of their time together filled her waking hours and haunted her dreams. She knew exactly how Sally felt about Greg, because she experienced that same bewildering sense of disorientation every time she tried to imagine spending the rest of her life without Steve. Instinctively she knew that, until she was with him, she would never feel whole again.

With a burst of feverish urgency, Megan got up from the table and ran to the phone. She had no idea how to get in touch with Steve, but Inspector Browning would certainly know. What if he had already been reassigned to another undercover operation? What if he had left for Afghanistan, or Outer Mongolia, or some other equally inaccessible part of the globe?

Her fingers trembled as she dialed Inspector Browning's personal number. Oh, God! How could she have been so crazy as to allow stupid feelings of pride to prevent her getting in touch with Steve before now? She fought to contain her frustration when a secretary informed her that the inspector wasn't in but that her mes-

Refuge In His Arms 173

sage—asking for Steve's current address—would be passed on to him at once. The inspector would probably call her back within the hour, the secretary promised.

In her present mood, an hour seemed an intolerable length of time to have to wait. She carried her cold coffee over to the kitchen sink, poured it out, and washed the cup under running hot water. She was rinsing off the last bubbles of detergent when the front doorbell rang. She grabbed a kitchen towel and wiped her hands as she hurried through the living room. Her fingers were still a bit slippery, and she fumbled with the heavy lock for a moment before managing to turn it.

She swung open the door, and her mouth widened in an inelegant gasp.

"You!" she breathed.

Steve Callahan pushed his tanned fingers through his soaking wet hair. The blond strands were already darkened by the pouring rain, and his raincoat was drenched. They stared at each other in silence, and then Steve's mouth quirked into a smile.

He reached out and gently removed the towel from her convulsive grip. "You were clutching a kitchen towel the first time I saw you," he said. "Do you always answer the front door holding a towel?"

She gulped. "No." She tried to say something more, but her voice had disappeared and wouldn't come back.

"It's raining," he said conversationally, as if she might not have noticed the torrential downpour. "Do you think I could come in?"

She gulped again. "Yes."

They walked into the living room and, with a supreme effort, she managed to produce a coherent sentence. "I thought you were in Washington."

His eyes brimmed with laughter. "No, I'm in Cambridge."

There was another moment of silence. Megan felt overwhelmed by the pleasure of seeing him again. She had forgotten the sheer physical impact of his presence, the impressive power of his broad shoulders, the startling attractiveness of his strong features and brilliant blue eyes the devastating charm of his crooked smile. Intensely aware of his attractions, she suddenly realized what she must look like: no makeup, hair all over the place, dressed in faded jeans and a shirt tied casually around her waist. She pulled at the ends of her shirt, trying to cover the two inches of bare skin around her midriff.

"Would you mind if I took off my raincoat?" Steve asked "I'm dripping on your living room carpet."

"It's not my carpet," she said, still too bemused by his presence to think clearly about what she was saying. "It's Jeffrey's." She swallowed hard, trying to order her jumbled thoughts and emotions into some reasonably intelligent pattern. "But of course you can take off your raincoat," she added hurriedly. "I'll hang it up in the kitchen; it should dry there."

Steve walked into the tiny hallway, shrugging out of the coat as he went. He hung it on the handle of the hall closet. "It'll be fine there," he said. He came back to her side, and all at once he was standing dangerously, hypnotically close to her. He put his hand under her chin, lifting her face up and searching her features intently. "How's it going, Megan?" he asked gently.

"It's going fine," she said. "Everything's just terrific. Couldn't be better."

"I'm glad." He glanced around the room, noticing the packing cases piled in the corner. "Why all the crates?" he asked. "Are you moving?"

"Yes, I'm moving out this weekend." She cleared her throat. "This house isn't mine, you know. It belongs ... it used to belong to Jeffrey. I'm clearing my things out and leaving the lawyers to fight about who owns the stuff that's left."

"Probably the government," he said dryly. His eyes glanced caressingly over her parted lips. "It must have been rough for you, Meg," he said softly.

His voice sounded warm and caring, tempting her to abandon the last stubborn remnants of her pride. For a breathless moment she hovered on the brink of confessing how miserably lonely the last two weeks had been. Then the habits of a lifetime intervened.

"Oh, things haven't been too bad," she heard herself say. It wasn't easy to confide your innermost feelings to someone when you had spent twenty-seven years concealing every trace of genuine emotion. She wanted to throw herself into Steve's arms and beg him to hold her. She wanted to say that her life was empty without him. What she actually did was to smile with artificial brightness and inject a totally false cheerfulness into her voice.

"Inspector Browning has been very helpful," she said.

"He's kept the press away?"

"Yes. And he arranged an appointment for me with a senior official in the registrar-general's office. That's the British government department responsible for recording births and marriages and so on. The officials there were very kind. They've already drawn up an official annulment of my marriage to Jeffrey Brookfield.

They decided that would be quicker and less painful than proving bigamy in open court. So now I'm legally Megan Richards again."

"That's outstanding news."

She looked up, startled by the unmistakable fervor of his tone, but before she could say anything, the phone rang.

"Excuse me," she murmured, picking up the receiver.

"Well, now, Megan, I hear you wanted to speak to me." Inspector Browning's friendly voice boomed over the phone. "How are you doing, young lady? Is the moving all organized?"

"I'm fine thank you, Inspector. I finished packing today, and I'll be moving out this weekend, as we agreed."

"I got your message," he said, his voice echoing with appalling clarity in the quiet of Megan's living room. "I understand you want to know Steve Callahan's address in Washington. The telephonist said you sounded as if you needed it urgently." He chuckled. "I've been wondering when you were going to come to your senses and admit you wanted to see that young man again."

Megan felt her face suffuse with vivid, embarrassing color. "I only wanted to write him a short note," she said quickly. "It wasn't anything at all important." She tried desperately to cut the inspector off before he could say anything too revealing, but while she was searching for a polite way to say good-bye, Steve came up behind her, and his arms lightly encircled her waist. Her heart began to thud so loudly she was sure Inspector Browning would be able to hear it, even on a long-distance call.

She struggled to retain her few remaining wits. "Well, thank you for calling so promptly, Inspector Browning," she said breathlessly. Anything else she had planned to

Refuge In His Arms 177

say died unspoken as Steve lifted her tangled hair away from her neck and began to trail his lips over her throat and shoulders in a slow, thorough act of seduction.

She gave an involuntary gasp of pleasure, completely forgetting to cover the mouthpiece of the phone.

"Megan, what is it?" said the inspector sharply. "Are you all right? Is somebody there with you?"

Steve reached out and took the phone from her nerveless fingers. "Yes, I'm here Sidney. I flew in from Washington this morning. And Megan's just fine—or at least she soon will be, now that I'm here."

Megan heard the inspector's rumble of laughter. "I see you got my message," he said. "I thought you'd be over here as soon as you knew Megan was leaving. What did you do? Wangle some compassionate leave on the grounds that you had to get married?"

"Someday, Sidney, your meddling is going to get you into trouble," Steve said, entirely without heat. "I'll talk to you later, you old reprobate, but for your information I don't *have* to get married. I just *want* to get married." He didn't wait for an answer, but hung up the phone with a decisive thump and turned Megan purposefully around in his arms. All trace of laughter had gone from his eyes, leaving only a burning, aching need that he made no effort to hide or disguise.

"Megan," he murmured, kissing her fiercely. "Don't make me wait any longer. It seems as if I've been dreaming forever of holding you like this." He leaned forward to kiss her again, clinging to her mouth as if he had been starving for the taste of her. "You're so beautiful, Megan. I think I've been half crazy from wanting you ever since I left Wales."

She twined her fingers into his rain-damp hair, hardly

able to believe Steve's words and her sudden, overwhelming happiness. "I know the feeling," she said with a husky groan of laughter. "Love me, Steve," she whispered against his lips.

He pushed her down onto the sofa, and she arched to meet the thrust of his body, linking her arms about his neck and parting her lips willingly to his kiss. Lying against the soft cushions, she luxuriated for a few moments in the familiar movement of his body against hers. She saw that his breath was coming in short, uneven gasps, and she felt a thrill of joy when she reached out to unzip his slacks and felt him shudder with pleasure.

He dragged his mouth away from her lips and pressed a row of hard kisses along her neck, trailing down toward the fullness of her breasts, pushing her shirt off her shoulders as he went. In two swift movements he tugged off her jeans, tossing them impatiently onto the floor as he rediscovered the pleasure points of her body with his fingertips. His lips burned kisses into her skin, arousing all the places that had yearned for his touch. His hands moved slowly down, tracing the shape of her breasts, her waist, and her hips, until her body blazed into exultant life, opening to his triumphant possession.

"Megan," he said. "Megan." He repeated her name, the word no more than a soft sigh in his mouth. "I love you."

"I love you, too." The words, once spoken, seemed so easy to repeat. She marveled that it had taken her twenty-seven years to learn how to say them. "I love you, Steve," she murmured as the thrust of his body carried her to a heart-stopping climax. "I love you."

* * *

A long time later she opened her eyes and smiled dreamily at him. "I love you," she said. With scarcely a pause for breath, she added, "I'm hungry, too."

Steve sighed. "I always knew you were a woman of highly romantic instincts," he said.

She propped herself up against the sofa cushions, a little shy as she looked at him. "I haven't been eating much the last couple of weeks," she admitted. "My appetite seems to have returned in a rush."

He touched her cheek, and his voice deepened to a throaty murmur. "Have I told you how much I missed you, Megan?"

"Yes, but tell me again."

"I missed you every minute of every day. Your face and voice haunted my dreams." He grinned with wicked charm. "And your body haunted my erotic fantasies, which — believe me — were becoming *very* erotic."

"Why did you let me go without telling me how you felt?" she asked suddenly.

His smile faded. "I'm sorry about that, Megan. But I was desperate to get away from you before I said something I thought I would live to regret. When Sergeant Davies arrived, he seemed like a lifesaver. I just wanted to get you out of the house — out of my life."

"Why, Steve? What had I done?"

"Nothing, except wind yourself around my heart so tightly that I was afraid I wouldn't be able to pry you loose. I was terrified of the power you had over me after such a short time, and I wanted to get away from you. I thought distance would help me put my feelings in a different perspective."

"I thought that, too," she murmured.

"Megan, you have to understand. My job has always

been the most important part of my life, and when I had to leave Luxembourg because my cover was blown, I was absolutely determined to get myself another undercover assignment somewhere in Europe. I knew that any permanent relationship with you would be the death blow to any hopes I had of reassignment to active duty. So I kept telling myself I didn't feel anything serious for you."

"And now?" she asked softly.

"And now I know how wrong I was," he replied. He gently kissed the tip of her nose. "By the time my plane landed in Washington, I already knew I didn't give a damn about being reassigned to Europe. All I wanted was to have you with me, sharing my life, giving it meaning and shape and purpose." His eyes darkened with a glow of tenderness. "I love you, Megan, more than I ever imagined I could love anybody. Will you marry me?"

She smiled radiantly. "Does tomorrow sound like a good day for a wedding?"

"It sounds fabulous," he said, gathering her close. "Oh, God, Megan, I'd forgotten just how fantastic you feel in my arms."

She curled her arms about his neck, straining against his body. He brushed a thick strand of hair out of her eyes, and his face grew tight with renewed desire. She ran the ball of her thumb across his mouth, and he nipped it gently with his teeth, and then their lips met in a long, explosive kiss.

When they finally drew apart, Steve's breathing was erratic. "We'd better get some clothes on if you're hungry," he said, standing up and retrieving her bra and jeans from the floor.

She sighed provocatively, but he turned away and

pulled on his slacks. "Let's investigate your kitchen cupboards," he said. "You look as if you could use a solid meal. I don't want my bride passing out in front of the minister."

They assembled all the ingredients they needed to make tacos, and while the ground beef was simmering with chili powder and tomato sauce, Steve poured out two glasses of wine and carried them to the kitchen table.

"Has Inspector Browning kept you up to date on all the details about Jeffrey Brookfield?" he asked.

"Most of them, I think." There was no pain left when she thought about Jeffrey. In fact, she realized that she didn't even feel very much interest. Jeffrey Brookfield was somebody she had hardly known, whose only lasting importance in her life was that he had brought Steve into it.

"The inspector mentioned that they've discovered Jeffrey's real name: Ilya Vasilevich. As you suggested, he was several years older than he claimed to be," Megan said. "He already had a master's degree in physics when he came over to England and enrolled in college. I guess he always planned to infiltrate one of the nuclear power projects."

"That's what I was told," Steve said. "I've been desperately busy these past couple of weeks double-checking the backgrounds of all the American scientists working on the Princeton fusion project, but so far we haven't come up with anything suspicious. It looks as if Brookfield and Meaney were working alone. Did you know Helen Meaney admitted that she was married to Jeffrey in the Soviet Union before they ever came over to England?"

For a moment a shadow crossed Megan's face. "Maybe

that's why he was so cruel to me," she said. "Maybe he felt uncomfortable living with me when his real wife was in an apartment just a few streets away."

"Maybe. But we'll never know for sure, and it's all over now, Megan. You don't have to worry about him anymore. That part of your life is over. It's finished."

"Yes, it is," she said, and as she spoke she knew that her words were true. The memory of Jeffrey's cruelty no longer had the power to hurt her.

Steve looked at her intently, then glanced at his watch as he lifted her wineglass to her lips. "Drink up," he said. "I estimate we have about ten minutes."

She swallowed a mouthful of wine, smiling with happiness as his eyes met hers across the rim of the glass. "Ten minutes for what?" she asked.

"Making love."

"But what about dinner! The tacos..."

"My dear love, you persist in seeing difficulties where none exist." He turned off the stove and put a lid on the simmering pan. "You see how easily I took care of your problem?"

Tears blurred her eyes. "Steve, am I really your dear love?"

"Yes," he said gruffly. He grasped her around the waist and swung her up into his arms, his lips brushing gently against her hair. "You are my lover, my companion, and my friend. You can rely on me, Megan. I'll always be with you, and I'll always love you."

She buried her face against the strength of his shoulders. "Show me how much," she said.

And he did.

WATCH FOR 6 NEW TITLES EVERY MONTH!

Second Chance at Love

___ 06573-0 **MIRAGE #61** Margie Michaels
___ 06650-8 **ON WINGS OF MAGIC #62** Susanna Collins
___ 05816-5 **DOUBLE DECEPTION #63** Amanda Troy
___ 06675-3 **APOLLO'S DREAM #64** Claire Evans
___ 06689-3 **SWEETER THAN WINE #78** Jena Hunt
___ 06690-7 **SAVAGE EDEN #79** Diane Crawford
___ 06692-3 **THE WAYWARD WIDOW #81** Anne Mayfield
___ 06693-1 **TARNISHED RAINBOW #82** Jocelyn Day
___ 06694-X **STARLIT SEDUCTION #83** Anne Reed
___ 06695-8 **LOVER IN BLUE #84** Aimée Duvall
___ 06696-6 **THE FAMILIAR TOUCH #85** Lynn Lawrence
___ 06697-4 **TWILIGHT EMBRACE #86** Jennifer Rose
___ 06698-2 **QUEEN OF HEARTS #87** Lucia Curzon
___ 06851-9 **A MAN'S PERSUASION #89** Katherine Granger
___ 06852-7 **FORBIDDEN RAPTURE #90** Kate Nevins
___ 06853-5 **THIS WILD HEART #91** Margarett McKean
___ 06854-3 **SPLENDID SAVAGE #92** Zandra Colt
___ 06855-1 **THE EARL'S FANCY #93** Charlotte Hines
___ 06858-6 **BREATHLESS DAWN #94** Susanna Collins
___ 06859-4 **SWEET SURRENDER #95** Diana Mars
___ 06860-8 **GUARDED MOMENTS #96** Lynn Fairfax
___ 06861-6 **ECSTASY RECLAIMED #97** Brandy LaRue
___ 06862-4 **THE WIND'S EMBRACE #98** Melinda Harris
___ 06863-2 **THE FORGOTTEN BRIDE #99** Lillian Marsh
___ 06864-0 **A PROMISE TO CHERISH #100** LaVyrle Spencer
___ 06866-7 **BELOVED STRANGER #102** Michelle Roland
___ 06867-5 **ENTHRALLED #103** Ann Cristy
___ 06869-1 **DEFIANT MISTRESS #105** Anne Devon
___ 06870-5 **RELENTLESS DESIRE #106** Sandra Brown
___ 06871-3 **SCENES FROM THE HEART #107** Marie Charles
___ 06872-1 **SPRING FEVER #108** Simone Hadary
___ 06873-X **IN THE ARMS OF A STRANGER #109** Deborah Joyce
___ 06874-8 **TAKEN BY STORM #110** Kay Robbins
___ 06899-3 **THE ARDENT PROTECTOR #111** Amanda Kent
___ 07200-1 **A LASTING TREASURE #112** Cally Hughes $1.95
___ 07203-6 **COME WINTER'S END #115** Claire Evans $1.95
___ 07212-5 **SONG FOR A LIFETIME #124** Mary Haskell $1.95
___ 07213-3 **HIDDEN DREAMS #125** Johanna Phillips $1.95
___ 07214-1 **LONGING UNVEILED #126** Meredith Kingston $1.95
___ 07215-X **JADE TIDE #127** Jena Hunt $1.95
___ 07216-8 **THE MARRYING KIND #128** Jocelyn Day $1.95
___ 07217-6 **CONQUERING EMBRACE #129** Ariel Tierney $1.95
___ 07218-4 **ELUSIVE DAWN #130** Kay Robbins $1.95
___ 07219-2 **ON WINGS OF PASSION #131** Beth Brookes $1.95
___ 07220-6 **WITH NO REGRETS #132** Nuria Wood $1.95

All of the above titles are $1.75 per copy except where noted

SK-41a

___ 07221-4 **CHERISHED MOMENTS #133** Sarah Ashley $1.95
___ 07222-2 **PARISIAN NIGHTS #134** Susanna Collins $1.95
___ 07233-0 **GOLDEN ILLUSIONS #135** Sarah Crewe $1.95
___ 07224-9 **ENTWINED DESTINIES #136** Rachel Wayne $1.95
___ 07225-7 **TEMPTATION'S KISS #137** Sandra Brown $1.95
___ 07226-5 **SOUTHERN PLEASURES #138** Daisy Logan $1.95
___ 07227-3 **FORBIDDEN MELODY #139** Nicola Andrews $1.95
___ 07228-1 **INNOCENT SEDUCTION #140** Cally Hughes $1.95
___ 07229-X **SEASON OF DESIRE #141** Jan Mathews $1.95
___ 07230-3 **HEARTS DIVIDED #142** Francine Rivers $1.95
___ 07231-1 **A SPLENDID OBSESSION #143** Francesca Sinclaire $1.95
___ 07232-X **REACH FOR TOMORROW #144** Mary Haskell $1.95
___ 07233-8 **CLAIMED BY RAPTURE #145** Marie Charles $1.95
___ 07234-6 **A TASTE FOR LOVING #146** Frances Davies $1.95
___ 07235-4 **PROUD POSSESSION #147** Jena Hunt $1.95
___ 07236-2 **SILKEN TREMORS #148** Sybil LeGrand $1.95
___ 07237-0 **A DARING PROPOSITION #149** Jeanne Grant $1.95
___ 07238-9 **ISLAND FIRES #150** Jocelyn Day $1.95
___ 07239-7 **MOONLIGHT ON THE BAY #151** Maggie Peck $1.95
___ 07240-0 **ONCE MORE WITH FEELING #152** Melinda Harris $1.95
___ 07241-9 **INTIMATE SCOUNDRELS #153** Cathy Thacker $1.95
___ 07242-7 **STRANGER IN PARADISE #154** Laurel Blake $1.95
___ 07243-5 **KISSED BY MAGIC #155** Kay Robbins $1.95
___ 07244-3 **LOVESTRUCK #156** Margot Leslie $1.95
___ 07245-1 **DEEP IN THE HEART #157** Lynn Lawrence $1.95
___ 07246-X **SEASON OF MARRIAGE #158** Diane Crawford $1.95
___ 07247-8 **THE LOVING TOUCH #159** Aimée Duvall $1.95
___ 07575-2 **TENDER TRAP #160** Charlotte Hines $1.95
___ 07576-0 **EARTHLY SPLENDOR #161** Sharon Francis $1.95
___ 07577-9 **MIDSUMMER MAGIC #162** Kate Nevins $1.95
___ 07578-7 **SWEET BLISS #163** Daisy Logan $1.95
___ 07579-5 **TEMPEST IN EDEN #164** Sandra Brown $1.95
___ 07580-9 **STARRY EYED #165** Maureen Norris $1.95
___ 07581-7 **NO GENTLE POSSESSION #166** Ann Cristy $1.95
___ 07582-5 **KISSES FROM HEAVEN #167** Jeanne Grant $1.95
___ 07583-3 **BEGUILED #168** Linda Barlow $1.95
___ 07584-1 **SILVER ENCHANTMENT #169** Jane Ireland $1.95
___ 07585-X **REFUGE IN HIS ARMS #170** Jasmine Craig $1.95
___ 07586-8 **SHINING PROMISE #171** Marianne Cole $1.95

Available at your local bookstore or return this form to:

SECOND CHANCE AT LOVE
Book Mailing Service
P.O. Box 690, Rockville Centre, NY 11571

Please send me the titles checked above. I enclose _____ Include 75¢ for postage and handling if one book is ordered; 25¢ per book for two or more not to exceed $1.75. California, Illinois, New York and Tennessee residents please add sales tax.

NAME _____

ADDRESS _____

CITY _____ STATE/ZIP _____

(allow six weeks for delivery)   SK-41b

NEW FROM THE PUBLISHERS OF *SECOND CHANCE AT LOVE!*

__ **THE TESTIMONY #1**		06928-0
by Robin James		
__ **A TASTE OF HEAVEN #2**		06929-9
by Jennifer Rose		
__ **TREAD SOFTLY #3**		06930-2
by Ann Cristy		
__ **THEY SAID IT WOULDN'T LAST #4**		06931-0
by Elaine Tucker		
__ **GILDED SPRING #5**		06932-9
by Jenny Bates		
__ **LEGAL AND TENDER #6**		06933-7
by Candice Adams		
__ **THE FAMILY PLAN #7**		06934-5
by Nuria Wood		
__ **HOLD FAST 'TIL DAWN #8**		06935-3
by Mary Haskell		
__ **HEART FULL OF RAINBOWS #9**		06936-1
by Melanie Randolph		
__ **I KNOW MY LOVE #10**		06937-X
by Vivian Connolly		
__ **KEYS TO THE HEART #11**		06938-8
by Jennifer Rose		
__ **STRANGE BEDFELLOWS #12**		06939-6
by Elaine Tucker		
__ **MOMENTS TO SHARE #13**		06940-X
by Katherine Granger		

All Titles are $1.95

Available at your local bookstore or return this form to:

 SECOND CHANCE AT LOVE
Book Mailing Service
P.O. Box 690, Rockville Centre, NY 11571

Please send me the titles checked above. I enclose _____ Include 75¢ for postage and handling if one book is ordered; 25¢ per book for two or more not to exceed $1.75. California, Illinois, New York and Tennessee residents please add sales tax.

NAME_____

ADDRESS_____

CITY_____STATE/ZIP_____

(allow six weeks for delivery)   **THTH #67**

WHAT READERS SAY ABOUT SECOND CHANCE AT LOVE BOOKS

"I can't begin to thank you for the many, many hours of pure bliss I have received from the wonderful SECOND CHANCE [AT LOVE] books. Everyone I talk to lately has admitted their preference for SECOND CHANCE [AT LOVE] over all the other lines."
—*S. S., Phoenix, AZ**

"Hurrah for Berkley... the butterfly and its wonderful SECOND CHANCE AT LOVE."
—*G. B., Mount Prospect, IL**

"Thank you, thank you, thank you—I just had to write to let you know how much I love SECOND CHANCE AT LOVE..."
—*R. T., Abbeville, LA**

"It's so hard to wait 'til it's time for the next shipment... I hope your firm soon considers adding to the line."
—*P. D., Easton, PA**

"SECOND CHANCE AT LOVE is fantastic. I have been reading romances for as long as I can remember—and I enjoy SECOND CHANCE [AT LOVE] the best."
—*G. M., Quincy, IL**

*Names and addresses available upon request